PRAISE FOR SUNDA

A classic of modern Tamil literature by Sundara Ramaswamy, winner of the Lifetime Achievement Award from the University of Toronto (2001) and the Katha Chudamani Award (2004)

"Reading Sundara Ramaswamy is like negotiating a minefield. Step on his stories, and something goes off inside your head. Not many can match the sheer thematic and stylistic range of his work and the enduring nature of his vision. Compelling and delightful, his stories have a strong feel for humor."

—*The Hindu*

"SuRaa pushed boundaries in both style and substance and was a master practitioner of the craft."
—"Nine Indian Authors Who Should Have Won the Nobel," *Swarajya*

"Perhaps, Ramaswamy's greatest accomplishment in writing a book of this nature is the fact that by the end, JJ becomes more an obsession of the mind; a wishful precedence takes over and you are left holding a void that Ramaswamy has conjured out of sheer imagination, the modernism from all of which is justification enough to read, reread, and read more of this wonderful writer."

—Firstpost on *JJ: Some Jottings*

THE
TAMARIND
TREE

THE TAMARIND TREE

SUNDARA RAMASWAMY

Translated by
Aniruddhan Vasudevan

Previously published as ஒரு புளியமரத்தின் கதை (*Oru Puliyamarathin Kathai*) by Tamil Puthakalayamin India in 1966, revised and published by Kalachuvadu Editions in India in 2001. Translated from the Tamil by Aniruddhan Vasudevan, based on the 2001 edition. The text was edited by Tashan Mehta working with Aniruddhan Vasudevan and in consultation with the author's children Thaila Ramanujam and S. R. Sundaram (Kannan).

Published by Amazon Crossing, Seattle

www.apub.com

Amazon, the Amazon logo, and Amazon Crossing are trademarks of Amazon.com, Inc., or its affiliates.

ISBN-13: 9781542034586 (hardcover)
ISBN-13: 9781542020657 (paperback)
ISBN-13: 9781428519367 (digital)

Cover design by David Drummond

Cover illustrated by Muhammed Sajid

Printed in the United States of America

First edition

THE
TAMARIND
TREE

1.

While it lived, the tamarind tree stood at the junction of three roads.

In front of it was a cement road that ran twelve miles to the south before vanishing into Cape Comorin, eager for a dip in the ocean. The second road, to the north, stretched past Thiruvananthapuram and Mumbai, perhaps all the way to the Himalayas, perhaps beyond that as well—after all, any place where mankind leaves a trail of footprints is a path, yes? The third road came from the west and split into two around the tamarind tree, before merging with the cement road. Who knows where this western path originated? In fact, isn't it simply the case that all roads begin at one coast and end at another? Then, in the middle, how can we talk of beginnings and ends? In truth, there were no roads that did not eventually lead to the tamarind tree.

It was quite an old tree and certainly looked it. From a distance, it looked like a hunched old woman with puffs of cotton for hair, her vision clouded over, and who, having transcended her desires, was now immersed in the hidden depths of her own bliss. When I first arrived in this town as a boy, the bus dropped me off at this tamarind tree. At the time, the junction was a busy market, full of rows of shops with every marvel. From salt to camphor, from the proverbial tiger's milk to elephant tusk, there was nothing that was not available! You could hold an engagement ceremony in the evening and conduct the wedding the very next morning, fully relying on these shops to supply everything you need in time. And in the center of it all was the tamarind tree— tall, proud, stately. How beautiful it looked that day, its canopy like hundreds of floating green umbrellas pulled together and held in place by a single rope. The whole scene had a glorious sense of harmony to it, of perfection, as if creation was pleased with its work.

Now the tree is gone. I firmly believe—and you may disagree—that no matter what we replace the tree with, no matter what wonderful new human invention we put in that spot, our town has lost its allure. Perhaps if we had left the tree alone, it would still be alive today, living in quiet dignity. But man, with his greed and chest-thumping bravado, killed it. How it happened is a story that is still fresh in our minds and will stay forever in our hearts. Some tales are impossible to forget.

Today—even though the tree no longer stands at the junction—cars, carts, and people still circle around the spot. They move around an absence. They must keep this up, if only in the interest of their own safety; otherwise, they'll collide with one another and create disaster. This is the tree's lesson for our town. But even those who have learned the lesson might feel embarrassed to admit it . . .

If you think about it, what crime did the tamarind tree commit? It only stood there, bearing witness to mankind's endless games. Did it actively participate in any? Did it care to? What did it do besides bear witness to man's laughter and tears and see how tears sometimes expressed themselves in laughter; or watch his selfishness or sacrifice and see how selfishness was mixed up with his sacrifice; or observe his jealousies and resentments and see how both of these were born out of love? In what way did it wrong humankind? Did it point fingers at anyone? Did it ingratiate itself to anyone? Did it conspire with any-body against anybody? It came to life on its own and was self-reliant in its growth. Leaves unfurled, then flowers blossomed, and then fruits appeared in such abundance that they hid the leaves from view. Old leaves fell to carpet the ground and merge with it, nourishing the tree that gave birth to them, becoming one with it. The tree's arms reached for the sky. Its roots wandered deep into the earth. It lived a simple life of contentment.

But when man is willing to gamble his country, money, women, power, and fame in his many games, why would he leave a mere tamarind tree alone? So he bet on it too and played one hell of a game.

This is the story of the tamarind tree's life and death.

Damodara Asan was at least eighty years old, but he claimed he was sixty-three. He did not want anyone to think, *Oh! He looks strong for an eighty-year-old.* Sixty-three, however, was believable. This man was immaculate. Even at his age, he could see well enough to thread a needle. Husking a hundred coconuts at a stretch posed him no challenge. Completing his daily five-mile walk was a breeze. His shoulders bulged out like palmyra fruits. Curly dark hair spread across the ridges of his wide back and chest and on the arm muscles that tapered toward his wrists.

He would often hold out his arm and say: "Here, try bending it. I challenge you. Any of you, come on, any of you old enough to have sprouted a mustache!" One by one, we'd hang from it, hoping to bend it. When it was my turn, he'd tease, "Oh, here comes the Brahmin boy, all resolved to bend my arm. Oh! He is going to crush it for sure. Aaaahhh! Sir, this is not a piece of spinach stem you are trying to bend!" I'd try and try, but I would always give up in the end, exhausted.

Asan was a philosopher, but nobody called him that during his lifetime. Humanism was his preferred ideology. He often used to say: "It is man who is Brahma; it is man who is Vishnu; it is man who is Shiva. There is no god beyond man—I do not believe in any power beyond humanity." We never paid much attention to his sayings; we did not really concern ourselves with philosophy. The only people we feared were our fathers, teachers, and the police.

Still, we idolized Asan. We followed him around like shadows, swarming around him, spending all our time with him. No father could bring himself to like Damodara Asan. No young man could dislike him. At home we were scolded for hanging around with Asan, and our teachers were visibly upset about it. Some nights, when we came home late after chatting with him, our families refused to open the doors, and we had to sleep on the front steps. Yet, enchanted, we always met him the next day.

There *was* a reason for our infatuation with Damodara Asan; it was not as if he had bewitched us with some magic potion. He was an incredible storyteller. How could one person carry around so many stories? So many stories, and such strange characters! With such crooked and twisted natures! We would listen to him for hours. Then, when we came home and slept, the thousand characters from his tales would rise up to dance in our minds. Asan's voice would whisper in our dreams.

And so each day after secondary school, we'd rush home, fling our books aside, and by five o'clock we'd all be walking down Asaripallam Road. That was where Joseph's laundry shop was in those days. Asan would be there too, sitting on a bench in front of the shop. He would always be in the same position. His staff—six feet long, thick as a club, steel-capped at the end—would be planted between his legs. His hands would be wrapped over one end, which came to a good two feet above his head, and the other end would be sunk three inches into the dust.

The moment he saw us, Asan would get up and start walking, his *veshti* folded so high that anyone could see his loincloth from behind. He never spoke when he walked. We followed him obediently, entertaining ourselves with idle chitchat.

We'd walk two miles down the road to the ruins of an old mandapam where they used to hang murderers in the olden days. The place still had this aura of a bygone era, as if we had leaped across half a century in just two miles. We often came across a madwoman there, always standing still, poised as if to jump into a swimming pool. She seemed to live in that mandapam.

Asan would sit in front of these ruins, and we'd arrange ourselves in a semicircle around him. Then one of us would humbly offer Asan a packet we'd purchased on the way and kept ready. Two stacks of Ittamozhi betel leaf, a dozen or so betel nuts, and two wads of Jaffna's Number One tobacco. Asan would chew the betel, spit it out, and glance around. Then, finally, with some unnecessary theatrics and grunts, he'd clear away the tobacco juice lingering in his throat. This meant that a story was about to start.

But Asan's stories never began in that well-worn style of our grandmothers. He never said: "Long, long ago, in a faraway land, there was a king . . ." Oh no. Asan had mastered the art of storytelling. He knew all its tricks and techniques. After staring intently at a nearby plant, he would say: "Does any of you know what plant that is?"

We'd peer at it, frowning.

"You don't know, do you? Hmph! I can tell from those stupid looks on your faces. All right. Crush two leaves in the palms of your hands and take a sniff. What does it smell like? Doesn't it smell the way new clothes stuffed in a coir basket for a long time do?"

We'd gape, awestruck. What a perfect description!

"You see," Asan said, leaning closer, "it was with *this* leaf that the wretched woman killed her husband. How could a woman bring herself to do such a thing? But then she had dared to desire another man. It wasn't that her husband was disabled. Or hunchbacked. Or blind. Or that he had found another woman on the side. Every harvest, give or take, he got no less than a hundred sacks of rice. He had enough to eat and entertain; every day at least a hundred banana leaves were thrown into the trash in his backyard. If you let his cattle out, it'd take half an hour to vacate the cowshed. One day he went to the Vadaseri market to find some bullocks for his cart, and he got two bullocks as sturdy as Arabian horses. He also bought some flowers for that damned woman to wear on her head. He thought she was offering him some milk to

5

drink, that's why he drank it. He vomited blood twice." Asan leaned back. "End of story."

This was how Asan set up his stories. Then he'd start chewing on betel leaves again. He was like a conjurer who offered a teaser, promising to show something thoroughly beyond our expectations, before he laid out his paraphernalia and got ready for the trick.

Later, the story would start from the poisoner's childhood. Her village, the people who had lived there, their relationship patterns, land ownership, marriage—all these details would be filled in. Just when the story got tense, he'd stop and chew his betel leaves again. We'd be left floundering, caught in the story, desperate to hear more.

Then the bell of the nearby parsonage would strike ten, and we'd realize how late it was. It was as if the bell's clapper had grown longer and was striking blow after blow on top of our heads, bringing us back to our senses. Home, mother, father, school, tests . . . Off we would run, back to our lives.

Damodara Asan is no more; he died even before the tamarind tree was destroyed. No one can tell stories like Asan did—one can only try. We heard all the old stories about the tamarind tree from him. He described what the area around the tamarind tree looked like fifty years ago, and what a glorious transformation had occurred since then. He took great pride in the fact that he had seen all those old sights, things we'd never see. How envious we were; we would have done anything to see those old places he described! Damodara Asan was indeed a very fortunate man. Yet *we* were lucky enough to know him. If we'd been born a few years later, we might never have heard any of these wondrous stories about our town and the early life of the tamarind tree. After all, historians don't write about tamarind trees. So perhaps we were fortunate too.

In those days, the tamarind tree was surrounded by a pond they simply called "the tamarind pond." Stagnant water reached down to incredible depths. At the pond's center, on ground that rose up like the back of a bathing elephant, was the tamarind tree, standing majestically with its incredible expanse of canopy and nodding its head. The little island-like mound was very narrow, just wide enough for two teams to stand close together and play a game of *kabaddi*. A little to the south of the tamarind pond were casuarina trees, swaying with a ghostly frenzy. They were so numerous and packed so densely that it was impossible to separate and hold a single tree in our minds. This casuarina grove was where local dawdlers went for their naps. To the east, lush paddy fields stretched all the way up to the point where the sky reached down to stop their advance.

Since there was water all year round in the tamarind pond, it was a convenient place for people's morning ablutions. But since moss spread over the surface of the pond like lotus leaves, there was not much of a stench. Still, the pond was mostly bereft of people for the rest of the day. Only curly-tailed pigs grazed happily. Back then, the main road was two miles away from the tamarind tree, winding through a longer route to its various destinations, so the area saw very few travelers as well.

But once the rains came and the grass grew lush and green, the cattle arrived to graze. The herding boys would drive them into the pond and give them a thorough wash, rubbing them with tender care. Then they'd drive the cows back onto land, and the boys would head straight for the tamarind tree. The elephant-like island mound would come alive with games, fights, and arguments. When twilight began to fade into night, they'd head back to town.

"Young girls didn't dare to head in that direction, not even by chance," Asan told us. "Old women came to gather cow dung, and little kids came. But not young women. They wouldn't even dream of being anywhere near the pond in those days."

"Why?" one of the boys asked in pompous Tamil. "Was it because sturdy young men waited there, ready to aim their arrows of love?"

"Nonsense! Earlier, everyone came to the pond. There was nothing unusual about it. But once they came to know what happened to

7

Kaliappan's daughter, Chellathayi, how could any woman dare to go there? A man showed up . . . No one knew where he was from, no one knew his name—in fact, no one had even seen his face. He dragged her by the arm, laid her down under the tree, and . . ."

Asan's story had begun. He'd told this same story many times before, and we'd all heard it, but we never got bored. He was ready to tell it again, and we were ready to listen to the story of Chellathayi and the moonlight stranger.

On her way home after a day of planting in the fields, Chellathayi fell out with her girlfriends over something trivial. She broke off from them and took the shortcut by the edge of the pond. It was the night of the full moon. The place looked enchanting. The pond was full to the brim after the heavy rains the night before, and the water lapped against the banks in little waves.

Chellathayi's excitement knew no bounds. She waded into the pool up to her knees and swirled the water joyously with her hands. She cupped water in her palms and poured it over her face. She took a mouthful and spat it out, as far as she could. She felt a sudden urge to have a proper bath, so she ventured farther. There was no one around as far as she could see. Right in front of her, a low-hanging branch of the tamarind tree sliced the moon in two. She savored this sight as she enjoyed her bath, making herself quite comfortable by removing her clothes.

Only when she began to shiver, her body having gone as cool as a banana stem, did she realize how long she'd been there. "Just one more plunge," she murmured, taking another dip. As she lifted her face above the surface of the water, she saw the tamarind tree in front of her. Even though the tree had always been there, and even though she was fully aware of this, she still found it incredible that a lone tamarind tree should be standing on a mound that looked like the back of a giant, sleeping elephant. She felt a sudden urge to swim up to the tree and back. So she slid deep into the water and started swimming.

When she stopped at a spot closer to the tree and looked around, she felt as if she had arrived at a distant and unfamiliar land. The casuarina trees swayed madly in the wind. Far off in the distance, the very field in which she had toiled from dawn to dusk now looked like a green shawl that had slipped from the shoulders of a hurried passerby. Her gaze drank in the landscape. She laughed in delight. Stretching her arms high over her head, she let the water trail down her body.

Then, suddenly, she heard footsteps behind her. She turned in alarm. A tall, powerfully built man stood there. He wore his hair in a knot at the back. Studs in his ears. A silk shirt. And his arms were long enough to reach his knees.

Her arms crossed and covered her chest. She couldn't speak. She stood, frozen. He gazed into her eyes for a few lingering moments. Then he walked toward her confidently, taking his time, and lifted her up as if he were lifting a child, carried her over to a spot beneath the tree, laid her down, and fell on top of her.

It took a few minutes before Chellathayi could find her voice. People sleeping in the casuarina grove heard her screams and ran to the pond as the stranger got up slowly, waded into the pond, swam to the other side, and emerged on the eastern shore. "Catch him! Catch him!" they yelled as they ran after him. When they got closer, he still did not start running. All he did was walk faster. Yet, incredibly, all their running could not match the speed of his strides.

I, Damodara Asan, was one of the people chasing him. I happened to be chatting with someone in the casuarina grove when the commotion started. So I ran after him too. If I had gotten my hands on him, I would have pounded him into dust! But even though he only walked, and we all ran, we still couldn't catch him. Can you believe this? How fast he walked!

Finally, once he reached the woods, he just vanished, leaping with great ease over a waist-high anthill as if he were jumping over a mere grinding stone. In all my life, I have never seen a man who walked with such agility and speed. And what a man! He was like a sculpture carved out of gold. His arms seemed to extend all the way down to touch the earth . . .

But what was truly perplexing was the change that came over Chellathayi. From that day on, she grew utterly infatuated with the stranger. She only had thoughts for him. She was tormented at night. At dusk, every single day, she came to the tamarind pond, swam across, and sat beneath the tamarind tree dripping wet, waiting for him. Later, she even started looking for him near the anthill now occupied by snakes.

The townspeople did everything they could to stop her. But she didn't listen to anyone. In fact, she acted as if what they said didn't concern her—as if they were talking about someone else. It got so bad that farmers would not let her work in the fields. They believed she was bad luck, that she would ruin the crops. But it did not bother her in the least. She simply stayed home. She did not care.

What a woman she used to be! Such a curvaceous body. She was so stunning. She had the beauty of good health, the beauty of youth, of flawlessness, of innocence. She was like a goddess. But now she'd become as gaunt as a plucked chicken. She did not want to eat rice or meat. The moment she took a morsel of food close to her mouth, she retched. Then she dropped the food from her right hand, pushed herself upright with her left hand, and walked away. All the women in the town came together to pray and make offerings on her behalf. They tied an amulet on her wrist. They performed rituals to ward off evil eyes. But nothing helped. She was wasting away.

Then, one day, the news started to spread that the man in question had visited her at home the night before. In fact, she said so to her friends.

After that, people started saying he visited her every full-moon night. But no one ever actually saw him. They only had her word for it, but they believed her completely. If they saw that Chellathayi had combed her hair, fashioned it into a bun, and worn flowers around it, then they were sure it was a full-moon night. On those days, she made herself wonderfully fragrant by applying sandalwood paste all over her body. The next morning, before the workday began, all her friends gathered at her house. Chellathayi delighted in telling them about the moonlight stranger's arrival the night before, his flirtations, his playfulness, his naughtiness . . . And her girlfriends sat around her and listened with desire in their eyes and envy in their hearts.

I once went to check on her, and she told me the whole story herself! She was absolutely unabashed in the language she used. It did not even occur to her that she should not be talking of such matters at all. When I listened to her talk of such things, even I became guileless . . .

Asan smiled wide when he said this, showing us his stained teeth. We tried to speed up the story. "What happened in the end? Tell us that quickly."

Some five or six months went on like this. Then one day she told her girlfriends that she was pregnant. And they believed her. No one had an iota of doubt about it. Ah! You should have seen how glorious she looked in those days.

"Was she beautiful?" we asked.

Oh, you can't just call her beautiful. We have seen beauty in many. But this was a whole other kind of gorgeousness. I don't know what to liken it to. Even those women who are most renowned for their beauty would have hanged themselves in shame. There was something special about her.

She really came alive. Her body started to grow more alluring than ever. Her friends who spent time with her every day could not believe the transformation. It had such an effect on them that they found themselves tongue-tied in front of her. They could not believe their eyes.

11

Her beauty filled them with shame about themselves, but there was not much they could do about it, only helplessly resign themselves to it.

Chellathayi was so excited about the baby. She got a lovely cradle made, and she even made baby clothes out of silk. Without any hesitation or embarrassment, she gave money to anyone who was going to the temple festival and asked them to buy wooden dolls and toys for the baby. It seemed as if she did not know how to express the surge of happiness in her.

Then one day, at the crack of dawn, the entire town woke up to her screams. People rushed to her side as she writhed on the ground, tossing and rolling in distress. The way she hit herself on the head was terrifying to watch. It was as if her skull was going to break into a hundred pieces. She was overcome. A cobra had bitten her husband in the screw-pine woods, she said. She had witnessed it with her own eyes. The snake had wound itself around his body from head to toe like the coiled and twisted rope of the temple chariot. It had clamped its mouth around his right foot, while its tail bored into his left ear. The whole town was alarmed. Armed with clubs and bamboo staves, twelve men set off and searched the woods thoroughly. But they could never find him.

The next day, we found Chellathayi's body hanging from a branch of the tamarind tree. She had fashioned a noose out of the very sari she was wearing.

2.

The day after Asan told us the story, we gathered outside Joseph's laundry shop. We showed up for days, then weeks, waiting for Asan to appear and finally finish the tale.

There was no sign of him at all.

Joseph guessed that Asan might have gone to visit his mistress in Sandanpudur, but there was no way of knowing this for sure. Asan was an enigmatic person—only his own shadow was privy to his movements. It was perfectly normal for him to vanish without a word to anyone, then appear several days later and carry on as if nothing had happened that needed explaining. If we had managed to learn anything about his private life, it was bits and pieces we had gathered from various sources, nothing more. The very same Asan who spun such fantastic tales for us never once, not even by mistake, gave us a fleeting glimpse of his own life story. It was just as Joseph often remarked—Asan's mind was like the secret chamber inside a Dindigul iron safe. We never got our hands on the key.

When Asan finally reappeared outside Joseph's shop, he looked terrible. Our storyteller appeared to be in the throes of some deadly fever. The sight of him—his body gone slack, his neck sagging, and his ribs poking out—moved us immensely. We put our heads together and tried, both directly and more subtly, to find out what had happened. But Asan evaded all our questions.

How withered he looked! The Asan we knew could stoically bear even the most heart-wrenching misery. We believed that as long as he had a hint of life in his throat to tell stories, a small audience to listen, and a roll of Jaffna tobacco to chew, even the worst sorrows would cower from him and run away. He was a fearless artist who had managed, by the sheer act of telling stories, to keep time's gaping void at bay. One could even say that he practiced the art of storytelling as his sacred duty till his last breath. So many poets in our country have been supported by patrons! (These patrons' poor taste and misguided generosity are quite evident when we examine the merits of some of those poets.) How could it be that there was no patron wise enough to embrace our dear Asan, pamper him with attention, and relish his stories for a lifetime?

We were shaken by the injustice of it. Quietly, careful not to draw Asan's attention as he sat on the bench in front of Joseph's shop, we emptied our pockets into a handkerchief behind the laundry table. One of us set off with a tiffin carrier to buy him snacks. Asan, who had pretended until then to not notice what was going on, shouted after him: "Also buy two Kalimark cheroots!"

Once Asan had the snacks and coffee we'd bought him, he looked much better. Contentment spread across his features as he lit the cheroot and took a puff. The way he shook his legs inside his veshti reminded me of how a calf wags its tail when it drinks from its mother's udder.

Pappu, who'd been sitting on a three-legged stool, moved over to the bench near Asan and stared at him.

"What is it, son?" Asan said with affection, putting his arm over the boy's shoulders.

"Asan, you left the story hanging and just vanished like magic," Pappu said. "You did not resolve the mystery of who that moonlight stranger was, the one with the ear studs and hair bun."

All this while, Joseph was pressing clothes on the long ironing table. Joseph had this lovely dark face and beautiful white teeth. Dark lips. A neat, crisp shirt—Joseph could not bear even a speck of dust settling on his shirt; half his time was spent turning his head this way and that and slapping away the dust on his shoulders. When he heard Pappu, he paused, holding up the iron box. "Who?" he said. "What's this about a stranger with earrings and hair bun?"

We summarized Chellathayi's story for him. While we were telling it, Asan kept staring at Joseph. As the story came closer and closer to the end, a faint smile crept over Joseph's dark lips. At this, Asan looked away instantly and fixed his gaze on the Ulakkai waterfalls—the pride of the northerly hills.

Joseph grinned, then winked at us. *Chellathayi's story is not true, it's invented,* his gestures seemed to suggest—but at that exact moment, Asan turned.

"*Dei!* You are undermining me behind my back?" Asan shouted, lifting his staff. "If you are a real man, challenge me to my face." Joseph smiled and seemed happy to, but Asan was not going to let him have his say. He planted his staff on the steps and entered the shop. "Hey! Look! What are you blabbering? Isn't it true that it was I who cleverly saved the tree from that wretched fellow's hands? Otherwise, do you think the tree would still be standing here? Tell me. If men and women and birds and beasts are able to enjoy its shade today, who is responsible for that? All the shops and businesses that rely on the shade of that tree today—tell me, who made it happen? Tell me, hand over your heart!" Asan slammed his hand on the ironing table.

"OK, fair enough," Joseph admitted. "What you said *just now* is true."

"What is?"

"If your plan hadn't worked that day, the tree would definitely have been cut down."

"So you agree?" Asan roared.

"I agree."

"Then shut your mouth!" Asan said, triumphantly.

"But I wasn't talking about that! I was talking about Chellathayi's—"

"You agreed, didn't you?" Asan said, cutting him off. "End the matter right there. Don't try to evade the facts."

Asan looked so smug and Joseph so resigned, we broke into howls of laughter. Asan joined us. Once peace reigned again, Pappu tried to get this *new* story. Who had tried to cut down the tree? How did Asan save it? But Asan wouldn't be rushed. We watched quietly as he took a packet of betel leaves from the folds of his veshti. We waited as he chewed, making sure we settled into comfortable spots.

"You all seem to think I am just making things up," Asan said. "But I am not lying. I am speaking of the things I have seen with my own eyes. If I had not intervened that day, the tamarind tree would surely have been felled. That damned fellow swung his axe with such force at the tree. Somehow something got me there at the right time. I stood behind him and grabbed his arm. Who did that? Me! What time was it? Two. Not two in the afternoon. Two in the *morning*. Who was cutting down the tree? Koplan, the priest at the Madaiyadi Maadan temple. His eyes were so bloodshot, they looked like freshly cut sheep thighs. He was totally drunk. Arrack. And he held an axe in his right hand. 'Wait, Koplan, wait,' I said, grabbing his arm. The moment he saw me, he froze—the raised axe just stopped in midair. I still laugh thinking about it . . ."

Asan started laughing at the memory of a petrified Koplan. His laughter grew until he was laughing with utter abandon, his eyes squeezed shut in delight, his back and shoulders shaking, his head rolled back. We exchanged knowing glances.

"You see, it was a tricky task. There was a chance my plan could work. But, on the other hand, it might not have, and I might have lost my head to his axe. After all, you don't know when death's coming for you, do you? It can snuff out life any second. But I decided to chance it. If I had not risked my life and flung myself in his way, that bastard would have cut down that lovely tree that day."

We could not stand the suspense any longer. "Who was it that came to cut down the tree?" we cried.

"I just told you. Koplan."

"—But why was he cutting it down?—"

"—How did you arrive at that spot at just the right time? Tell us that first!—"

"—Why do you do this, Asan? You tie up the story in so many knots, we are at a loss! It's like being abandoned blindfolded in a forest."

Asan laughed with glee at having spun us in circles. But he picked up the thread again. "Remember I told you that Chellathayi hung herself from the tree?" he said.

"Yes! Yes!" we cried like little children.

Asan leaned his weight on his right hand planted firmly on the bench, tilted his head to the side, squeezed his lips with the fingers of his left hand, and spat out a long stream of tobacco juice. Then he grunted to clear his throat and told us the story of Koplan's revenge.

)(

It turned out that Chellathayi's family came to know of her suicide only after the cowherd boys informed them after dark. Poor Sornam. She hitched up her sari and ran the entire three miles. When I, Damodara Asan, saw her and Kaliappan running and overtaking each other, I wondered what the matter was. I too hurried in the direction—not that I had anything else to do!

You see, it was pitch-dark by then. Only bats went near the tamarind pond at that hour. Or foxes that came down from the northern hills. Or crawling insects. If you saw a person headed there at that hour, you could be quite sure that he had lost all regard for his life. But I was not scared. Why would *I* be afraid to go? Things were different in those days—there was some respect for people's qualities and values. At the very mention of the name "Asan," even a cobra would relent and drop its hood . . .

We exchanged glances. Asan cleared his throat twice and wandered back to the real story.

17

Kaliappan and Sornam were under the tamarind tree, shrieking and sobbing in grief. I collapsed against a casuarina tree. If only you had heard the way Sornam sobbed and wailed that day. *Ammadi!* Every word she uttered wrung my heart dry. She held up the loose end of her sari and appealed to God. She hit herself repeatedly on both her cheeks. And I don't care if you believe me or not when I say this—I shed tears too.

I walked up to the edge of the pond and looked at the tamarind tree. From one of the lower branches, something hung and swayed in the wind. It looked like a doll the masons hang to ward off the evil eye from new buildings. At the sight of it, I broke out in a sweat all over my body. All I could think was how good it would be to have some light in that moment. Anything. Even a small matchstick would do.

Then I heard a commotion behind me. A brisk crowd from Keezhacheri was headed in my direction. One of the men was balancing a long ladder on his head. A man in the front of the crowd and a man at the back were carrying a plantain tree each. Ahead of everyone was a little boy leading the way, carrying a lantern, alternately walking and running despite his limp. They were clearly headed to retrieve Chellathayi's body. As soon as they saw me, someone yelled, "Who's there?" I spun in circles twice right on the spot, clapped my hands over my head loudly, and ran zigzag, shouting all the while. They just laughed at me and went their way.

From there I headed straight to the clock tower and stopped for tea at bowlegged Shanmugam's shop—you know Pechi's son from Erachakulam? I finished my tea and was on my way home, smoking my cheroot, when I saw Koplan the priest hurrying ahead of me. His thick curly hair stood straight up over a foot above his forehead. Streaks of holy ash covered his body. A large vermilion mark shone on his forehead. On his waist, he wore a veshti in garish red silk. And he held an axe over his shoulder. I could tell from the way he walked and the crazed look in his eyes that he was up to no good. I followed him discreetly.

18

You see the kinds of disruptions that keep a man from getting a decent night's sleep? What can I do? It is my fate. The policeman who draws a regular salary gets to sleep comfortably on a canopied bed every night, his arm over his wife next to him. But *I* am supposed to roam around at night, keeping watch! *I* am supposed to catch the thief, stop the smuggler, and intercept the runaway girl and get her back home. It is on *me* to catch the coconut thief in the act or spy on the local big shot who drapes a shawl over his head and frequents the alleyways! The kinds of sordid tasks that fall on me! But what can you do? All you can do is to think of it as your fate and go along.

Koplan suddenly vanished into the casuarina grove. I looked toward the pond. The scene I witnessed there is still etched in my mind. The ladder came floating along in the water, like the temple float at the Suchindram festival. On it, Chellathayi lay stretched out. Near her head was balanced a lighted lantern. And the bad-legged boy sat close by with a look of sheer terror on his face. It was a pathetic sight, I tell you.

Even in that state, how beautiful she looked! All I could see were her face and those breasts that stood out like two firm guavas. One moment her hair fell over her face in the breeze, and the next moment it moved away gently. There was no life in those poor hands to even move the hair from over her face. And she was devoid of all modesty, that wretched woman, even to cover her chest. How lovely she used to be. Such an arresting presence she had. When she swayed her hips and preened like the temple peacock, every man felt her spell. If an old man on his deathbed happened to catch a glimpse of her, he was sure to tear up at the thought his life had been wasted. Men devoured her with their eyes. The silly whore ended it all in one second. Who would want to go near her now?

For a little while, I stood watching them carry away that ladder with Chellathayi's body laid on it. Then I looked toward the casuarina trees.

The priest was nowhere to be seen! How could he have vanished so quickly? I walked toward the southern bank of the pond. I saw a figure—Koplan!—jumping into the pond and swimming toward the tamarind tree. I could not imagine what business anyone could have at that time of the night with the tamarind tree. What was this Koplan doing? It suddenly occurred to me that this hapless fellow might also be planning to hang himself from the tree.

Then I heard the sound of an axe hitting the tree. The blighted fellow was cutting down the tree! What hubris! Did they all think that Asan was dead and gone?! That they could just cut down that tree?! Was this tree planted by Madaiyadi Maadan, your deity? Or did they think their father planted and watered the tree? I was too agitated to stay quiet about all this. So I jumped into the pond right away.

Asan took out a cheroot from the folds of his veshti and lit it. He pursed his lips and blew out smoke in intermittent puffs. Then, with a great show of effort, he hacked up a fake cough, drew in his stomach, cleared his throat, and spat forcefully. Then he turned to us.

I swam to the mound, climbed onto it, ran, and grabbed Koplan's arm. He turned and glared at me. And I stood there, glaring right back at him, without blinking even once.

"Is it you, Asan?" he said.

"Yes, it is indeed Damodara Asan," I replied.

"Asan, don't meddle in this. There is no saying what I will do right now. Move away."

I raised my voice. "Oh yeah? What will you do?"

"I am here to cut down this tree. If you try to stop me, I don't have a problem cutting you down first," he said. He lifted his axe over his head—

Asan paused. We leaned forward, spellbound. The silence was too heavy to bear. Then he continued, his voice now soft and dangerous.

"So how long have you been planning to compete with me like this?" I asked him.

"Why would I compete with you? You think I am crazy or what?"

"Not crazy. Arrogant. Hey! Do you know that no one has ever dared challenge Asan?"

"You are the one stopping me from cutting down the tree."

"Why would I stop you? I have been planning for a long time to cut down this blighted tree myself, but I had to figure out the right day and time for it. And here I am to do the job. You think you can steal the moment from me?"

He was thrilled when he heard that I had come to cut down the tree too. "What do you mean? What are you talking about?" he asked over and over.

"Do I have to repeat myself? Are you hard of hearing?" I shouted.

"You have really come here to cut down this tree? Truly?"

"No. I have come to shave your head," I said.

"Asan!" he shouted, and fell at my feet.

At this point in his storytelling, Asan changed voices; he grew understanding, pliable.

"Aren't you Muthu's son, from Keezhacheri?"

"Yes, yes, that's right."

"Son, do you know who made sure your father got the lease for the Isanimangalam field from Emden Iyer?"

"My father told me."

"What did he tell you?"

"That it was you who got it for him."

"And did you know that it is only since then your father has been wearing those red-stone ear studs?"

"Mmm."

"Did you know that it is only since then your father could afford some meat to his meals?"

"Asan . . . ," Koplan said, shivering with gratitude.

"Not just that! It is I who got him the land lease that allowed your father to replace his thatched roof with new tiles."

"Asan, please. Please don't humiliate me anymore."

21

"You loathsome fellow! You were about to bite the hand that embraced you? You decided to light the funeral pyre for Kaadukotthan Pichuva's entire family? Hmm?"

"Forgive me, Asan! Please forgive me!" the boy screamed, and fell at my feet again.

The boy wouldn't let go of my feet. I asked him to get up, but he wouldn't. "Tell me you forgive me. Only then I will get up," he said, and held my feet firmly.

I put my arm over the boy's shoulder, gently led him away from the tree, and sat him down.

Koplan asked me: "Asan, why do you want to cut down this tree?"

"Son, take a good look at this tree. Do you know what it is?"

"It's a tamarind tree."

"You think this is some regular tamarind tree? You fool! It is poison through and through."

"You are absolutely right, Asan!"

"So you had the same plan, then?"

"Yes."

"To get rid of it and all the evil that goes with it?"

"Yes."

"Did the deity command you? In trance?"

"Yes, in trance."

"Was there a festival?"

"Yes."

"When?"

"Last month."

"It was Sangili, wasn't it?"

"Yes."

"What did the deity say?"

"That I had to cut the tree down."

"The command was only for you, no one else?"

"No. Kattai Subbaiya too."

"The same command?"

"Yes."

"How come he is not here?"

"He is scared."

"He is scared!"

"Yes."

"Why?"

"He is scared."

"Koplan!"

"Asan!"

"You are not an ordinary fellow. I was wrong in my judgment of you. It is clear that the deity makes itself known to you."

"That's what they say in the village," Koplan said, proud.

"So you have a good reputation."

"Initially only people in the nearby villages knew. But now it's spread even farther."

"You are Kaadukotthan Pichuva's grandson after all! You were born to do great things for your family! You have made a name for yourself. I am really happy for you. Pichuva and I were close, did you know that?"

"I have heard."

"You are in his thoughts. That's what has brought me here at this hour, mind you. I am here because he called out to me and said—*My grandson is in some serious trouble, go save him.*"

"Why do you say that, Asan?"

"Koplan!"

"Asan!"

"Koplan, I feel bad looking at your face. You are just a child. Pure as milk fresh from the cow. The deity commanded you, and you proceeded right away with an axe to fulfill it. You thought you could cut the tree down and swim back ashore, didn't you?"

"Yes. Why?"

"Of course that's what you'd think. That's what they'd want you to think. Don't be scared. I will tell you. After all, that's why I have been brought here at this hour. Koplan, if you had cut the tree down, you would have thrown up blood and died right here on the spot."

"Asan! What are you saying?"

"Koplan, look, this tamarind tree? It is evil for sure. There is no doubt about that. Evil spirits wander here. They strike the goats that graze here. They kill the cows. I cannot even begin to tell you how much I have wrestled with these spirits."

"Can that be true? Is there any spirit that you cannot control?"

"There is one fiery spirit living in this tree. Let me tell you how he operates. He does good to good people and harm to the bad. If you act insolent around him, he will rip you to shreds. You see, this evil tree was going to cause some serious harm to the whole of Keezhacheri. This fiery spirit was able to put that off by offering Chellathayi as sacrifice. Anger is a sign of virtue. It was about to tear you to pieces. But you got out alive."

"Asan, I am feeling so agitated," Koplan cried out pitifully.

"There, there, son, don't be afraid. It is insulting to me if you feel scared when I am here. There is a solution for everything. And I am going to teach you a way out."

"Tell me, Asan. Tell me, please!"

"See, we are in a tight spot at the moment. This tree contains both good and evil. Like mating snakes, they lie intertwined. We have to tease apart one from the other carefully, the way a swan separates milk and water. But let me tell you one thing clearly. If we are afraid of this tree and we go away now leaving it as it is, we are done for. We need to maim it. It is like cutting off a girl's nose just when she has come of age and is all ready for marriage."

"Tell me what to do, and I will do it."

"Koplan, do one thing. Cut down the branch from which that poor girl hanged herself. That will be the end of it."

Koplan did as I asked. Within the next fifteen minutes, one of the branches cracked and fell down. The two of us picked it up and threw it into the water.

"Dawn's breaking. We'll invite trouble if we stay here any longer," I said, and jumped into the pond. He jumped in right after me. Once we got ashore, he headed south and I went north.

In the end, it was I who saved the tamarind tree. If I had not acted shrewdly that day, the tamarind tree would have been cut down right to the roots.

X

Asan's story was over. Something in him changed when he finished it. His face hardened, and it felt as if the bond between him and us had snapped.

"Asan," Pappu asked, voicing what we were all thinking, "why was the fellow in such a rage to cut down the tree?"

"Pappu, imagine you have been fantasizing all your life about marrying a girl. Then if another man shows up one day and whisks her away, tell me, won't you feel furious?"

"He and Chellathayi . . ."

"Yes! Yes! He was her maternal uncle's son. But the poor fellow was unlucky. After all, she was no ordinary treasure. It takes a special kind of luck to get such a woman. So he was angry. And the man needed something on which he could vent out his anger and jealousy and disappointment, didn't he? If he took it out on a fellow human being, he'd be in trouble with the law. If he beat up somebody's cow, he'd have to answer to the owner. But here stood a lone and mute tree. So he sharpened his axe and set out to settle his score with the tree."

"Why couldn't you have given us this bit of information earlier?" asked Tiruvaazhi.

"Oh, wow!" Asan said irritably. "How does it matter when I tell you?" He rolled up his towel and lay down in a huff, resting his head on the makeshift pillow. We looked at each other, uneasy.

"But one thing simply must be said," Joseph declared, loudly and wholeheartedly. "If Asan had not come up with his plan that day, the tree would have been cut down to its roots!"

But Asan showed no sign of having accepted the compliment. He had already closed his eyes.

One by one, we said our goodbyes to Joseph and headed home. I kept thinking about the story of Koplan. In losing a branch, the tamarind tree had ensured its survival. It was an excellent plan. Isn't it the smartest thing to do—to give up something in exchange for self-preservation? Even a madman is basically someone who has given up his intelligence in order to protect himself, isn't he? A lizard has its tail to lose, a woman her honor, a man his principles, and God His mask. Losing and gaining seems to be essential for survival. To lose a bit of yourself, to gain a bit of something else, and to absorb into oneself what was gained in order to protect oneself from destruction—to ensure one's survival in times of crisis—hasn't that always been what religions have done, what civilizations have done, what languages have done? It seems to be the law of nature.

The tamarind tree stood bereft of a branch. With the branch went its shadow. Even the wound at the spot where it'd been cut soon healed and turned into a scar. But after that, in time, the tamarind tree sent forth new branches. The branches extended out, the tree's shadow grew bigger, and the crowds that arrived there for the shade grew bigger too. The tamarind tree seemed unperturbed by everything, offering its excellent shade to innumerable people.

Yet nothing grew at the spot where the branch had been cut. Not a single shoot, leaf, flower, or fruit. Nothing.

3.

Years had passed since Asan told us the story of Koplan's revenge. I'd graduated from secondary school by then and even left town for a new job. I ended up being tangled in a love affair (love indeed!) that greatly humiliated me, and I had to come back to town without a job and my head bowed in shame. The less we say of it, the better. I met with so much mockery and ridicule wherever I went in town, I rarely left the house. Even men who covered their heads and loitered in the back alleys sniggered at me. *Let them laugh,* I told myself bitterly, *it will do them good.*

But this meant I never ventured out of the house before seven or seven thirty in the evening. Like shards of a coconut smashed against a rock, all my old friends had scattered away to other towns after school. The pressures of earning a livelihood had dragged them away in all directions. I was alone. But how long could I stay trapped in the house? When it was dark enough for me not to be recognized on the streets, I'd wrap a shawl around my neck and head out west, the cool wind soothing my face. I always headed to Joseph's laundry shop.

For a long time now, I had dwelt on Asan's stories of the tamarind tree. One question in particular fascinated me—how did the tamarind pond transform into the tamarind-tree junction?

When my family left my father's ancestral village, taking everything we owned to this town where my mother was born, it was at the tamarind-tree junction that we first arrived. I will always remember the first time I saw it. Oh, the junction was the town's heart, the crowning glory of the market! Day and night, it buzzed with life, crowds thronging the streets at all times. It was as if hundreds of thousands of beehives had been disturbed all at once and now there was a steady humming buzz in the air, a million racing pulses. On these streets, children automatically clutched their elders' hands more firmly, and even adults felt comforted by this move.

And I? When I first stepped off the bus, I was overcome. Here we were, in this busy town, having come from a little village where every car drew gawking crowds. The bright lights of this junction, in a neat sequence here, a little disorderly there, stretching as far as the eye could see, the flashy storefronts, the waves of crowds, and the vehicles that crawled bumper to bumper—and the sounds! The hustle and bustle of the crowds and the immense sound the tamarind tree made when it was rocked by the roaring wind. I was awed.

So ever since Asan began telling us these stories about the tree, I wanted to know this story in particular. How did the pond become the junction? I knew that transformation had occurred during Asan's lifetime, so I was desperate to hear the story from him. However, it was no mean feat getting Asan to talk about the things we wanted to hear. God alone knew how his mind worked! He was a wild stream; you couldn't hold him in the palm of your hand. Besides, Asan had grown tired of talking about the tamarind tree. Yet another of his peculiar ways, I surmised. He sometimes developed a sudden aversion to the very subject he was in the middle of detailing with so much zest; he'd drop it suddenly and move on to a different topic. No one could fathom the reason for these caprices of his mind. Who knew; perhaps it was my own excessive interest in the tamarind tree that had turned him off the subject? People are full of strange quirks, and Asan was a confluence of eccentricities.

Those were our last days with Damodara Asan, and they were really something! His stories were outstanding, his skills at their dazzling best. Perhaps if I had been less of a scatterbrain then, I would have preserved these stories better. But life and the demands of making a living possessed my mind like a deadly spirit so thoroughly and crammed it with so much muck and trash, there was no room left for Asan's treasures.

Still, even though I have forgotten several of Asan's stories, this one I remember.

)(

Asan was sitting cross-legged on the bench outside the laundry shop, looking somber. With his walking stick, he was poking at the pieces of coal that lay scattered in front of the shop. There was a narrow stool close to the doorway. As long as you sat on it carefully and with some humility, you could balance well enough to avoid tipping over. I stationed myself there.

Joseph was pressing clothes on the long ironing table. He was a committed socialist; in his shop, right above where he stood, hung a picture of Achyut Patwardhan, a freedom fighter beloved for his socialist ideals. Today, Joseph was prattling on about something to Asan. He was describing his revolutionary plan to give the British a twelve-hour notice before sending them packing in their ships. Asan, however, was of the firm conviction that only royalty and white men were fit to rule, and that they should certainly be the ones doing the ruling. He sat in silence, his face growing redder. It must have been hard for him to listen to a novice rambling on like that in his presence.

At an opportune moment, Asan deftly snatched control of the conversation and hoisted his flag of authority. He spoke loudly of the kings of old. He expounded with great flourish on the heroic deeds of those kings. When his speech arrived at Maharaja Pooram Tirunal, the king of the princely state of Travancore, he spoke with the utmost adoration. He raved about the king's mastery over the arts, his fearless heart, and how he protected his subjects like they were his own children. Joseph couldn't stand it. He interrupted Asan and said, "Now you listen to

29

me, Asan. You are talking about their royal lineage. It is not very long before they will have to learn shorthand and typewriting just to keep their bellies full! Just you wait and see."

That was all it took. Asan was absolutely incensed.

"*Dei*, Joseph! What utter nonsense! What do you know about their family? You were born yesterday, but you run your mouth like you know everything," he shouted. Joseph shouted right back at him, but Asan was not going to give in so easily. "*Dei!* Listen. This place used to be nothing but a feeding ground for vultures. Every day four people were put to the stake here. What was so great about this town? The tamarind pond stank so badly that no one could come anywhere nearby. Weeds had grown rampant everywhere. Jackals howled even during the day. If they attacked a lone passerby, there was no one around to help. Why, even this spot where you have your shop now? Do you think anyone coming here in those days could avoid getting bitten by a snake? One breath from that pure and righteous Maharaja Pooram Tirunal fell on this place, and lo!" Asan snapped his fingers dramatically. "This cremation ground of a town turned into heaven!"

I gestured discreetly to Joseph to shut up. A story about the tamarind pond was imminent, and I was anxious to hear it. But Asan had turned his face away in mock anger. We had to buy him a cup of tea and a packet of betel leaves, areca nuts, and tobacco before his temper cooled down a bit. Even then, only after both Joseph and I pleaded with him a few times did he relent. Grudgingly, he cleared his throat in preparation for the story.

Asan began his story by declaring that the reign of Maharaja Pooram Tirunal was the most illustrious period history had ever seen. There was no Sanskrit text that the king had not studied. He was an expert in philosophy, scripture, astrology, medicine, everything. He had abundant affection for his subjects, and he was a gentle soul.

"When I say the king was a gentle soul, I totally mean it. He was the gentlest soul. Mind like a child's . . ." Asan burst out laughing. Then he quickly pursed his lips and looked up at the awning in an effort to control himself, but he couldn't. He burst out laughing again.

"Look at him laughing! What is making him laugh so hard? He can't control himself!" said Joseph.

"Back in those days, there was another story about him. But I don't know if that was true or not," Asan said, laughing again.

"Well, if you tell us that story, we can join in the laughter too!"

This was, apparently, the go-to story for anyone who wanted to make a point about how guileless the king was. One day, Maharaja Pooram Tirunal went to watch a football match. The sport was new to the kingdom then. Less than ten minutes into the game, tears started streaming down the maharaja's face. All the officials and guards around him panicked, wondering what had offended the king. But none of them had the courage to ask him directly. Eventually, the maharaja's private secretary, Sthanunatha Iyer, approached the king and stood respectfully in front of him.

"Sthanu," the king asked, shedding more tears, "has our kingdom fallen on such hard times? What is going on? Why are twelve grown men fighting over a single ball?"

Asan never told us whether the maharaja was reassured or if the football game continued, but I had the feeling that every player got his own ball that day. Gradually, after we'd all stopped laughing, Asan returned to the story about the maharaja, the tamarind pond, and the mysterious smell.

※

It was customary for the king to head twice a year to Kanyakumari for a dip in the ocean. It was an age when people possessed a tremendous loyalty toward the king, times when no one was certain whether the king was God incarnate or God was king in divine form. Once they knew that His Highness was making a visit, it was all anyone could talk about.

It took six months of preparation for each royal visit. And as soon as the king had left a place after a visit, preparations for the next visit would begin right away. Every year, all year round, preparations were always afoot for the king's tours of victory. Roads would be mended. The king only took proper ceremonial baths, so new tanks were dug in every place he stayed, and all tanks, old and new, were filled with fresh water. On the day of the king's visit, every schoolchild was given a special snack and every poor child was given new clothes.

It was quite an extraordinary sight, the maharaja arriving in a golden chariot pulled by six horses. The diwan's chariot always followed the king's, but with only four horses, and it was only a silver chariot. The diwan could look at the crowds as much as he liked, but the crowds wouldn't look back—they had eyes only for the maharaja. The maharaja would pass by, hands pressed together in front of his chest, nodding graciously to the people gathered on both sides. He'd keep this up until the end—hands together and nodding to the crowds. Soon after he passed by, people would argue among themselves. "He looked straight at me." "No! He was looking at me!"

At the time of our story, only the eastern section of the town existed. Even the main road was about two or two and a half miles away to the east of the tamarind pond. It was late summer. The west wind, known to be quite vigorous, had just begun to blow. It would blow dust in great swirls. All the piles of waste lying on the ground would rise up in the wind and hang in the air like giant palatial pillars for a few seconds before scattering back to oblivion.

The day Maharaja Pooram Tirunal visited our town, a strong west wind was blowing in full force.

Maharaja Pooram Tirunal had spent the previous night at the grand palace in Vadaseri and now was making his way to our town. To welcome him, the fireworks started at four in the afternoon. A river of people stretched from Vadaseri all the way to Ittamozhi. Children, young folks, the elderly . . . The entire street seemed awash in gold and silk. At any other time, if anyone had given even the most accurate inventory of the variety of clothes and jewelry that the women of this town owned, no one would have believed them. Visitors from out of town still kept pouring in. So many faces, such a variety of jewelry, so much laughter, such dazzle! It was all utterly magical! And the excitement in the eyes of all those waiting by the sides of the road! The eyes looked like they were ready to pop and fall out!

The royal procession was approaching Minakshipuram. A silence fell upon the crowd. It was so quiet, people could hear themselves breathe. Now the maharaja had arrived in front of the Vadivamman temple. The temple bell rang. When the king stood up in his chariot and brought his hands together in prayer, people could tell his devotion from the flutter of his eyelashes.

Suddenly, the west wind began to blow with great force and brought with it an unpleasant smell. The smell was quite faint at first, but very soon people were exchanging glances, their faces grimacing in disgust.

The wind grew fiercer, lifting the loose ends of women's saris like boat sails. All the decorations hanging in the storefronts were ripped off and collapsed in heaps.

By now, no one could disregard the foul smell on the wind. It stank like all the fish in the sea had washed ashore to rot. The retinue of royal officials did all they could to bring the situation under control. Bonfires of incense sticks were burned. They lit a ritual fire and cast fragrant substances into it. Yet no matter what they did, the thousands of noses could smell nothing but that stench. Sthanunatha Iyer, the king's private secretary, stepped down from his brass chariot and called the officials every colorful name in the book. But who had the power to order the wind to stop?

The king made a humongous effort to keep his poise. His plan was to keep smiling as if everything was fine. He tried to smile at everyone. But it was too cruel an ordeal, and he could not bear it any longer. Besides, he had a sensitive nose that had never experienced anything like this. When even ordinary people who were blessed with everyday experiences of bad smells could not bear this one, how could a king?

In seconds, his smile vanished and he grew dark with anger. His face contorted. Indeed, it was most unfortunate that his face began to look like it was the very source of the horrid smell. He had taken *such* care to set out at an auspicious hour, even making sure two Brahmins crossed his path for good luck. What else can we call it but the cruelty of fate that those two Brahmins had collected their fee and were now eating nice hot food in some dining hall that served free food to Brahmins, while here was the maharaja, only halfway through his journey and caught in such a predicament? The king had had enough.

"Drive on!" the maharaja shouted. The horses surged ahead, swift as the wind. According to the original plan, the maharaja was not expected to arrive at the Suchindram Palace until nine at night, but now he and his procession got there by five.

At midnight, the tahsildar of our town, Muthamperumal, sat in front of the Suchindram Palace, wide awake and holding his head in his hands. Preparations for the king's visit were the responsibility of the town tahsildar, and this visit could not have gone more wrong. Everyone was of the opinion that Muthamperumal's prospects now looked rather bleak. He had hired a bullock cart and hurried to the palace as fast as he could, hoping that he could meet the maharaja right after his dinner and before he went to bed; he would fall at the king's feet and beg his mercy. But when he arrived there, he only met Sthanunatha Iyer. He held Iyer's hands and beseeched, "Please save me!" The general belief was that Sthanunatha Iyer's words carried great influence in the palace. The maharaja happened to be a bit of a pleasure-seeker—and everybody said that Sthanunatha Iyer's wife was an incredibly beautiful woman, the kind of beauty that deserved to be captured in a painting.

After his excellent dinner, the king was seated on the swing. His silk shawl had slid down from his shoulder and lay draped over his hand and his thigh. Lounging on the swing, he pushed it with the big toe of his left foot touching the marble floor, doing so with such delicateness that it seemed he was anxious to hurt neither his toe nor the floor.

Sthanunatha Iyer entered the room, followed by Muthamperumal, who was half hidden behind Iyer. As soon as the maharaja glanced at him, Muthamperumal quickly took off the towel from his shoulder and tied it around his waist. Then he prostrated at the maharaja's feet, making sure that his big toes, abdomen, and forehead were all pressed against the floor. When he stood up, the king's feet as well as Muthamperumal's cheeks were both soaking wet with tears.

The tahsildar tried to speak, but he found he could not say a single word. His mouth had gone completely dry. He was drenched in sweat so thoroughly that he looked like he had taken a dip in the pool with all his clothes on.

Sthanunatha Iyer began: "Muthamperumal says it was all a mistake . . ."

But the king cut him off. "Sthanu, you don't have to say anything. Just listen to me. You see, roses have a particular smell. And jasmine has its own fragrance. Mullai has a totally different scent. I knew that there were different kinds of fragrances, and I have experienced many as well. But while I knew that, I had assumed until today that all bad smells were of the same kind! If I stay shut up in the palace all the time, how could I expect to know how my country smelled? If my palace smelled wonderful, did that automatically mean my kingdom smelled wonderful too? Please thank this tahsildar on my behalf. What a variety of smells he has introduced to me!" The maharaja laughed thunderously as he said this, but his face and eyes grew red.

The two men stepped outside. Neither of them could say with certainty whether the king's words had been reassuring or ominous.

They found out the next morning. The order came straight from the king: Muthamperumal was given the sack.

Poor Muthamperumal! What could he have done? He had arranged everything perfectly. He had not had a proper night's sleep in three months. He had even lost ten pounds. Despite all that, he still lost his job. What could he have done in the face of nature's mischief?

Who could have predicted that the tamarind pond would become the reason for all this chaos? When they flooded the ponds in the region with fresh water, how did they overlook the tamarind pond? Did they assume that the pond had nothing to do with the king's visit? Did they overlook it because it was nowhere near the main road? Was it ignored because it kept to itself? It might be an old pond, but it was still a pond, no? The water was filthy, but it was water nevertheless, wasn't it?

But they had indeed ignored the stagnant cesspool that was the tamarind pond. The water in it was filthy: its surface covered with moss, sludge and slime in its depths, human waste scattered all around it. It had been the source of the stench and had played its ominous part in the maharaja's visit. Everyone conceded that even an old pond had a few powers of its own. A mere fetid pool had managed to drive away the king. And Muthamperumal's livelihood had been sacrificed to its wrath.

The next day, all everybody could talk about was the emergency resolution issued by the maharaja. Apparently, His Highness had arrived at this decision when he was in Kanyakumari. In the temple, in front of the deity! He declared that on his way back a week later, he would travel right by the tamarind pond. So they only had a week—just seven days—to fix the pond.

Orders flew in all directions. Overnight, a plan was devised to drain the tamarind pond and then fill it up with soil. With assistance from a British engineer, an Indian engineer submitted a plan that would cost a hundred and fifty thousand rupees. Only God knows where they managed to find such a flood of people to put to work. Officials from the court headed in all directions; they went from town to town to hire laborers, and they brought back thousands of men and women. The government issued an order, effective immediately, that all construction work within a fifty-mile radius had to be halted for two weeks. Every cart in the area was stationed near the tamarind pond. As a result, even the farmers' market was canceled for two weeks.

They dug a sluice to drain the water from the tamarind pond into the Therekalputhoor channel. In just a day, the tamarind pond merged with the Indian Ocean. Then they stacked up and burned sandalwood all around the pond, in preparation for the main work.

There was a hill about four miles south of the tamarind pond, just by the foothills of the Maruthuva Mountain. They called it Pariah Hill. The entire hill was sheer red earth that had piled up over eons in the space between two mountains. Half as tall as a palm tree, it looked like a giant anthill. Thousands of workers now arrived to dig up and carry soil from this hill. I sat perched in a tree and watched how a basket of the red earth from the top of the mound was passed through several pairs of hands before it was emptied into the open cart parked by the road-side. By the time the hill was leveled to the ground, there was not even a trace of the tamarind pond left. With gashes on their necks from all the beatings and feet swollen from all the work, the bullocks collapsed. The pond had been filled up in just two days.

Then, for the next four days, they focused on laying the road. It ran in a straight line from Vadaseri to Kottar. This new road passed right in front of the tamarind tree. All the commotion around the pond had not affected the tamarind tree in the slightest.

On its return journey, the maharaja's golden chariot passed right over the spot where the tamarind pond had been. The entire area was filled with the scent of the flowers that lay scattered all over the road. The place looked absolutely heavenly.

"If the maharaja had not come that day, nothing would have changed about this place. The western section of the town would not have developed at all if they had not laid the road! That's right: it was only since his visit that this town has come into its own," Asan finished.

Neither Joseph nor I was particularly impressed by this story. We felt that Asan was exaggerating things just to bolster his argument. It was my opinion that it did not take a king's visit for a town to improve and develop. But I did not say it out loud; I did not want to get Asan all riled up again.

Perhaps Asan realized his story had not gotten the reaction he'd expected, because he simply got up and left—started walking away, without a word. I can still see it, the way Asan waddled away in the dark, folding up his veshti so high that anyone could see his loincloth from behind. It would be the last time I saw him.

A few days later, I finally got an offer for a new job and moved out of town. When I returned two years later for my wedding, I learned that Asan was gone. I was chatting casually with Joseph when he gave me some shocking information about Asan. Apparently, Asan had gone with a rich man to visit the Kataragama Murugan temple in Sri Lanka. He never came back. At first, the story was that he had tricked a rich Sinhalese man by promising to perform alchemy and that he had been charged for fraud and thrown in jail. Another version was that he had contracted cholera and died by the seaside. Just before his last breath, he was supposed to have said in a clear, loud voice, "There is no God." Joseph told me that Asan's mistress, that woman from Sandanpudur, showed up from time to time at his shop, cried her heart out, and took some money from him for her ride back home. She'd told Joseph that she had in her possession the skin of the tiger that Asan had shot with his own hands.

To me, someone like Asan could not die so easily. As long as we remember his stories, and as long as the people who hear his stories from us remember them, he lives in some way.

𝕏

Over time, I heard from others how the big market emerged in front of the tamarind tree and how the western section of the town developed.

It happened slowly. When the tamarind pond was first filled, heavy carts rolled by day and night over the road that passed in front of the tamarind tree. It was by this road that goods from the warehouses in Kottar went to towns in the east and west. What used to be the tamarind pond was now leveled ground—it became a playing ground, of sorts. There, in the evenings, boys played kabaddi and ball games. One side of the playground turned into a parking area for carts at night, and cart owners could be seen unyoking bullocks for a night's respite from pulling travelers. When bus travel became prevalent, the playground turned into a bus stand, and a few shops and food stalls cropped up around it.

Gradually, traffic increased. The road that passed in front of the tamarind tree was now paved with cement. The area became a "junction." Even though there were many other junctions and tamarind trees in the town, when people spoke of "the tamarind tree," this was the tree they meant, and when they mentioned "the junction," they were talking about this one. When the number of vehicles on the road increased exponentially and the traffic became uncontrollable, they shifted the bus stand and the parking area for carts to a different location.

The playground area—which had once been the tamarind pond—was once again empty, and so the municipality proposed a development project. Based on that proposal, comprehensive plans were laid out for a first-class shopping area around the tamarind tree. The playground area was divided into small plots and individual leases were drawn. Neelakantan Potri, who came from Udupi, built a two-story building and started a restaurant. Initially, he had to spend over a lakh of rupees, but gradually over the next ten years he did very well. He then bought twenty acres of prime irrigated land near the Putheri Reservoir. A dozen or so of his taxis roamed through town. He wasted no time in buying up all the empty lots in the vicinity. They say that years later, when he grew old and decided to return to his hometown, he had to be paid twenty thousand rupees over and above the cost of construction just to convince him to vacate his lease.

Next to the restaurant, and right in front of the tamarind tree, a row of stores sprang up. The shop nearest to the restaurant was a money changer, next to that was a barbershop, and next to that stood a snuff dealer (wholesale). Right across the road from the tamarind tree was Abdul Khader's famous stationery shop. Next door to it was the big movie theater, which was always packed and busy.

At the center of it all was our tamarind tree. Power lines brushed the top of its canopy. Telephone lines too. The string of lights crisscrossing the storefronts and rooftops looked like someone had sliced up a bolt of lightning and rearranged it back in space. By five in the evening, the tamarind-tree junction was buzzing with crowds. A single hour at the junction was equivalent to spending ten years living in the town. Just standing there you could witness the town's highs and lows, its charm and its filth, all in one place. The junction brought so much wealth and change, there was no end to the number of housing colonies that kept springing up to the south of the tamarind-tree junction. The people who moved to the town from elsewhere had a difficult time finding a place to live.

Yet, no matter how much the town changed, the tamarind tree was just the same. People stuck advertisements on its trunk. Tattered movie posters hung from its lower branches. Flags of all political parties fluttered from its limbs. The tamarind tree stood there, enduring it all, involved in nothing. No one even paid attention to the tree any longer. But they were saying its name all the time, for every little thing. *Tamarind-tree junction.* They might have forgotten the tree, but they still had to utter its name.

Asan had once spoken with pride about how he had served the human race well by saving the tree. It was true, as far as he was concerned. But even today I am not able to say with certainty whether the tree's survival that day was a loss or a gain. I know about all the tragedies that followed. Asan didn't—he had simply used the standards of his own times as a yardstick to calculate gain and loss. When you consider everything that happened later, perhaps it might have been better if the tamarind tree had been destroyed that day. After all, wasn't the tree the very reason for the quarrels, arguments, disputes, and animosities that followed?

But perhaps we cannot say this with certainty. When man is hell-bent on taking the path of ruin, nothing can stop him.

4.

When the tamarind-tree junction was still the tamarind pond, there used to be a grove of casuarina trees to the south of it. Once upon a time, this grove was steeped in darkness. Like a pair of bellows, it constantly hissed haughty gusts of air. Anyone who lost their way and found themselves at this desolate place was overcome with a sense of emptiness and dread, and they quickened their steps, walking away as briskly as they could.

But to Asan, the casuarina grove was comparable to heaven. It was an experience of utmost delight for him to spend time alone in the grove, the lone inhabitant of the kingdom of solitude, watching the casuarina trees' rapturous dance. The sight must have kindled Asan's peculiar taste in things. He always said he was more entranced by the terrifying face of Kali—the goddess of time and death—than by the gentle goddess Kanyakumari. If he found petrol lying spilled, casting its liquid rainbow on the road, he'd stop to take in the smell: "Ah! What a pleasant smell," he'd say before walking away. He once told us: "Everyone keeps saying the same old things, that flowers are fragrant, that sandalwood is fragrant. But the scent that hits you when rain drizzles on red earth when it's all dried and cracked and dusty—ah! Looks like only snakes and I have the proper sense of smell."

It was no surprise, then, that the casuarina grove pulled at him like a magnet. Whenever Damodara Asan spoke about the casuarina grove with great fondness, he seemed like a child turning its favorite candy in its mouth over and over, anxious to make it last. "Aha! The darkness there is so cool and comforting," he said. Apparently, he'd been there innumerable times in the past to sleep off heavy meals. "Especially if I have gorged on a proper wedding feast, complete with vadai and pradhaman, then the next thing I know the casuarina grove would tug at my feet. Once I go there and collapse, that's it. When I wake up, I have to ask someone to find out what day it is."

"It was quite windy there, wasn't it?" someone said, spurring him on.

"*Dei!* Don't call it wind; call it a breeze," Asan said. "Aha! What a wonderful breeze! It was like being stroked with pure silk. It was like baskets and baskets of jasmine flowers showering on you," he said, stacking up similes.

It was from Asan that we learned about the casuarina grove—how, in the full heat of the day, even with the sun beating down overhead, it cleverly kept a little bit of the night trapped within itself.

Asan told us that the grove had been there even when he was a little boy. But he could not tell us if the trees were packed so densely by nature or if someone had planted them that way. No matter how vehemently we pursued a point, he'd never admit he didn't know the answer. "Why do I care about all that? All that mattered was it was a fine place for a game of cards," he said, evading the question. But he was right. For nearly fifty years, young men from our town—as well as nearby towns—went to the casuarina grove for their early lessons in habits that would quench their minds' appetites. Card games, ganja, alcohol, pornography, the Kama Sutra, symptoms of sexual ailments, their cures, stories of legendary whores—every casuarina tree in the grove has borne silent witness, watching and listening, as young men learned these things. Those simple trees must have been shocked and terrified by the deviancies of human minds, by our endless proliferation and perversion of desires.

Asan told us that, just as the morning sun started to bear down, the herding boys would arrive with their flock and drive the buffaloes into the tamarind pond. Then they would head off into the casuarina grove and turn the place upside down with their antics. They particularly enjoyed climbing the trees like monkeys. While the branches of the trees became smooth as the boys' palms rubbed against them, the boys' hands grew blistered and cracked like the branches had been—Asan was great at such naturalistic descriptions. I also remember Asan saying that, as the boys got used to leaping from branch to branch and tree to tree, in time they developed their own favorite pathways in the air, so much so that even when they jumped with their eyes shut, branches would appear magically to receive them.

If they grew tired of being monkeys, the boys played ball games, or if they were in a really jubilant mood, they stripped off their loincloths and threw them under the tree, wrestling and rolling together on the dusty ground. After all, modesty is just a consideration we show others, isn't it? Moreover, it was not in the nature of that place or the friendship between these boys to demand conventional modesty. If they wanted, they could freely shout out obscenities, and if they had the imagination and penchant for word conjugation, they could generate a string of new abuses; they could even come up with new and delightful ways of uttering these curses! It was only natural that these young minds were curious about sex and procreation. Every so often, teachers would emerge from within their midst and clear away the boys' ignorance by undoing the knotty mysteries of creation with precision and clarity. The boys had questions about many such things. In fact, I must say that it was in the casuarina grove that a lot of children had their questions cleared up. It was convenient that the place had the tranquility that is always absolutely essential for the exchange of knowledge.

Now the grove of casuarina trees is gone, and in its place is a municipal park. The way the place is today, after the modern fashion, casting enchantment with its shrubs and creepers and the cool moonlike glow of the fluorescent tube lights . . . Asan would never have set foot in this place if he were alive—I am absolutely certain of this. I wouldn't be surprised at all if Asan had hurled his choicest abuses at the municipal chief responsible for making this park. In any case, the grove's transformation can offer a flash of insight into the whirling wheel of time to even those who are a bit slow or clouded in their vision.

When the casuarina grove transformed into a municipal park, it was very different from those old times Asan used to describe. By then, the tamarind-tree junction was bustling with life. The tamarind pond had vanished, the bazaar had come up around the tree, and the bus stand to the south had already been built. The place was absolutely chaotic with the noise of the traffic and the jostling crowds. In that new and modern setting, the casuarina grove might have appeared out of place, much like an unfashionable piece of jewelry on a young college girl. You could say that time had transformed tastes so much and so quickly, it had become possible for someone to actually think, *If only the casuarina grove were not here . . .* and relish that possibility.

It is true that many had come to think of the casuarina grove as an eyesore, but the credit for actually making this declaration goes to our municipal commissioner, F. X. Fernandez. When he won the election and announced that his first task as public servant would be to destroy the grove to build a park, everyone applauded him. He proclaimed it was just the first step in his elaborate plans to transform our town into a modern city.

Municipal Commissioner F. X. Fernandez's enterprising nature ensured that the grove was soon destroyed and the park built. In doing so, he found an everlasting place in people's hearts. Asan took leave of this world before witnessing the grove's wondrous—or I should say hideous—transformation into a municipal park, but I got to see it.

It is still fresh in my mind—watching from the side as the casuarina trees toppled. My friend and classmate Chakrapani Rao was the one who dragged me there forcefully to watch it happen. The trees fell down one after the other, their trunks buckling and screeching. In the shock and impact of the branches crashing and shattering against the ground, the tree would rise up slightly in the air before falling back on the earth with a thud. The place looked like the corpse-ridden battlefield of Kurukshetra after the Mahabharata war. The pathetic sight of a lone tree lying on the ground reminded me of the loneliness and misery endured by a widow. I stood there and watched it all, but I was distressed.

I kept thinking of Asan. He had described with pride how he had cunningly intervened to save the tamarind tree from being cut down. How painful it would have been for him to witness hundreds of axes working in unison to fell a tree a minute! There was a difference, though. This time it was not one man's action. It was an order from the highest office of the government! A government that had been elected by the people for the people. In such an arrangement, where the instincts were embedded in everyone's pulse, who could challenge whom? Even so, if Asan were alive, he would have tied up his veshti and jumped into the fray for a fight, not realizing how much the times had changed.

But in today's world, wouldn't all of Asan's impressive tricks and his bravado be completely rattled by even a simple question from an ordinary young man? What could Damodara Asan reply if such a young man said to him, "Asan! If you are unhappy about the casuarina grove being razed, you have every right and freedom to contest and win the next election, demolish the park, and turn it back into a grove . . ."? Wouldn't Asan feel absolutely tongue-tied? Even if he got into a point-less argument with the man, what could it accomplish besides exposing to the world Asan's backward mindset and outdated principles? No matter how smart Asan was, how could he understand the language this young man was speaking? Eventually Asan would realize one thing. He would realize that those days of democracy that Joseph had once pre-dicted while ironing clothes in his laundry had arrived. All Asan could have done in the face of these transformations was to vent his anger by hurling a few fistfuls of earth at the world and cursing it to his heart's content. It was just as well that he had died during his own time.

However, it would be incorrect to say that with Asan's death, his ways of looking at the world vanished as well. One particular instance comes to my mind. An elderly Nadar who had been watching the destruction of the grove in shock tapped the young man standing next to him on the shoulder and said, "Young man, why on earth are they cutting down the trees?"

"They are going to plant some shrubs here," the young man replied.

"Why do they want to plant shrubs?" the old Nadar asked.

"For some breeze."

"And shrubs will provide more breeze than the trees did?"

"Well . . . to make the place more beautiful," the young man said, changing his answer.

"So only shrubs are beautiful?"

"Mmm."

"Won't the shrubs grow into trees?"

The lad looked at the old man. Then he said with impatience, "They will plant only the kinds of shrubs that don't grow into trees. Or they will keep them trimmed."

"I see, they will keep them trimmed?"

"Yes."

"What idiots!" exclaimed the old man. He followed that up with some choice abuses. His indignation was evident in his flawless diction and perfect enunciation. His face glowed with satisfaction at having found more evidence for his firm belief that the world was hurtling down the path to ruin. I saw Asan's face that day in that old man's questions and his perfectly rendered abuses. The Nadar looked nothing like Asan, of course, but that was Asan's voice, no doubt.

So it seems that the murmurs of these voices will always persist in the background. But these are lonely voices. Has the world ever stopped in its tracks to pay attention to these mutterings? The plans for revolutions unfolding in the back rooms of time will leave everyone behind. Even the revolutionary can't seem to keep pace with time; he becomes the object of mockery for new revolutionaries. But when a little boy flies his kite and lets the string run rapidly through his fingers in his delight at the favorable wind, it is the tail that keeps the kite from flipping over by pulling it down slightly with its weight.

The trees were felled, and glorious sunlight usurped the space now emptied. The darkness that once lay tethered to the grove was now gone. The glare was too much for the eyes. It was as if a thousand canopies had been taken down and suddenly there was a dazzling rain of molten silver.

The work on the park advanced at a great speed. Thousands of men and women were engaged in the task. A young man from Thanjavur arrived to take charge of things. He'd been abroad to study landscaping. It was clear that his pre-agreed two-year salary was going to strip our already impoverished municipality to the bone. But then people whispered that he'd been on his way to Italy, and it had taken strong convincing to get him to agree to offer his services to us instead. The work proceeded entirely under his supervision. First, they cleared away the dusty sand and leveled the ground. Then they spread some moist soil and planted grass all over. They made flower beds, and winding walkways, and planted colorful hedges bordering these paths. They erected trellises and introduced rare creepers to climb over them. Exotic varieties of plants were imported from overseas. There could be no room here for commonplace flowers like rose, jasmine, and the like. In fact, it felt as if all flowering plants were to be treated with contempt.

They created a decorative pond at the exact center of the park. It had a novel shape, and its appeal seemed to rely entirely on the fact that no one could find any correlates in nature for it. Painted rubber ducks floated in the pond. And how much more beautiful than real ducks they were! There were fish in the pond too. The decorative pond was cleaned every day to make sure no moss formed on the surface, and a watchman was appointed to keep people from spitting into it. They even fed tinned food to the fish twice a day.

A section of the park was turned into a tiny zoo. Elephant, bear, duck, deer all stood on display. What an accurate depiction! And all so green! That young man—the one from Thanjavur, wearing thick glasses and long white pants, his dense hair neatly combed and pressed down—would frequently consult a heavy leather-bound tome he carried in his hand and shout commands. Right away, the workers who stood at the ready with colossal shears clipped away at the places he pointed to. The young man remained focused on his task, now walking up to the topiary for a closer look, now receding to look at it from a distance, then giving it a direct look from the front, then bending his knee to view it at an angle, squinting at it, and consulting his leather-bound volume again before issuing more commands to the workers bearing giant shears. It required daily meticulous supervision, that green zoo. If he was not careful, the female elephant might grow tusks and turn into a bull, or the deer might put on too much weight, or the duck might spread out its plume and dance like a peacock, or some other such indecorous thing might occur. The plan to craft beauty carefully might fail miserably.

There was no end to the wonders that young man from Thanjavur performed in our town's fancy new park. Flowers blossomed only in the colors he commanded. He made running creepers fold into tight curls. He made even small plants grow long drooping leaves just as he wanted them to. He had everyone amazed at the way he put creation to utter shame with his science.

In another corner of the new park, the radio was always on full blast. At first, the people who gathered in the evenings for gossip found this noise an intrusion. But in time, they grew used to it, and now the sound became the background score for their gossip sessions. In the evenings, there was not enough room on the grass or on the benches to accommodate the crowds that flowed into the park. Both men and women came to the park. It was very rare to see lovers together, but newlyweds showed up within a week after the wedding. The park was among the few places they were eager to experience in the early weeks of their marriage, since they rightly suspected that they might not get to do these things later.

The way the women flirted, lying on their stomach, chin propped up with a hand, feet lifted up to greet the starry skies, and smiling at their lover's face; then, overcome with shyness, letting their eyelids droop before fixing their gaze on the grass; and then laughing with abandon, their shoulders shaking—it was all exquisite! When they stretched one arm in front and lay their head over it, and when they gave the impression of being tired, their eyes growing languorous as they slid their body down gracefully—the feminine charm that shimmered in those fleeting new gestures was absolutely enchanting. I don't think such gestures have ever before been within the reaches of ordinary femininity. Sometimes, in very much the modern fashion, the loose end of their sari slipped from their shoulder. No matter how often a woman pulled it back up over her left shoulder, the sari was far too mischievous to stay put! Young boys and girls walked around the park, selling sundal, roasted chickpeas, roasted green peas, and groundnuts. Women flirtatiously lit their husbands' cigarettes. The bra straps that were prominently visible over their shoulders and on their broad backs through their translucent blouses held men's eyes in thrall. Some of the new ways of casting sidelong glances were utterly merciless. They dragged your mind away in a fierce wave and crashed it against a rock until it shattered into a million glass pieces. You felt the urge to spit in the face of the spiritual disquiet that arose in that moment.

There is no law that said only retirees could sit on the benches around the decorative pool. No sign had been put up to that effect. However, in the course of time, it was as if that spot had been officially written over to the elderly as their special entitlement. Faded umbrellas and frayed walking sticks were forever slipping off the benches there.

In fact, that entire spot—the benches, the plants and creepers, the tube lights, and even the pool—seemed to have aged a great deal. Also, was there no end to the elderly's complaints about the weather? Wind and rain, breeze and drizzle, mist and sun, cold weather and chill wind—if nothing agrees with you, what can anyone do about it? Some of them started sneezing the *moment* the weather report announced possible rain for the coastal areas! When vehicles passed by, blazing their horns on the bazaar road, these people were visibly distressed by it. They were convinced everything in the world was conspiring to torment them. They looked around with such innocent faces, they could melt even a stone to pity. They constantly blamed "Kaliyugam" (the end-times) for all that was wrong with the world. They scrutinized the modern young women who passed by the park, then muttered disapprovingly that both women and their femininity had been too exposed. When cars and trucks passed by, leaving clouds of exhaust in their wake, these elders rushed to cover their noses and mouths, pulling their white shawls with their pale, parched fingers. Once the dust settled, they took a pinch of snuff with an irritated snort. They fell back into memories of the past, reminding each other of those lovely, long-gone days when all was well with the world. On days when one of their Letters to the Editor appeared in the English newspaper, they argued about it with gusto.

When these retirees got together in the evenings, they asked after each other's health. Their list of dietary restrictions seemed to grow longer by the day. They compared these lists and felt either jealous or happy. They seemed to think that if God was unable to distribute happiness equitably, then He should at least be impartial when handing out suffering. They imagined how wonderful it would be if they could start life over, combining the wisdom of their present years with the youth of their past. In an effort to hide their colossal failures, they showed off their small victories, but when this foible was exposed and the truth became known, they were too embarrassed to even look at each other's faces. But still they laughed. And since they ended up coughing if they laughed too hard, they laughed as hard as they could without cough-ing. They never tired of laughing together at their stale old joke: *If a person does not have blood pressure or diabetes, they are not allowed to sit on the benches around the pond.* This much is evident from the way they talked—for all the great disappointments that He had dealt them, if God could at least grant them quick and easy death as a lucky prize, then they were ready to forget all His betrayals and praise Him for His compassion. Whenever one of their peers drew the winning ticket for a quick and sudden death, they earnestly prayed: "God, me too, please."

In one corner of the park stood a memorial pillar for Gandhiji. Some of his famous sayings were etched on it in the most formal Tamil. The municipality appointed a caretaker to stop people from climbing up the memorial stairs with shoes on and to drive away people who sat smoking near the base of the pillar. In true Gandhian spirit, this man was dressed in a khaddar khaki shirt.

From the lawn, one heard reviews of both English and Tamil mov-ies. Solid, serious discussions. Even the intricacies of cinematic tech-niques were analyzed in detail. The evening editions of the dailies had created buzz about a famous Tamil actress's miscarriage. Some of the college boys sitting in the grass were worried about her. They sent a reply-paid telegram inquiring whether her bleeding had stopped. In fact, one of their group was stationed outside the telegraph office. These boys were anxiously awaiting his arrival by bicycle, and they were look-ing around impatiently. The oldest among them reminded everybody of the advances in medical science, trying to reassure himself as well as the others. Their conversation also revealed that the actress endured this physical ordeal just two days after giving a remarkably realistic performance as a woman in labor for a movie scene. Their concern for her made them a tad pious and philosophical, and they started saying things like "God always subjects the righteous to tests" and "Bad things always happen to good people." If you looked at their somber faces, you would feel that you too must summon your inner purity and pray for the actress's bleeding to stop.

Loud commentaries on political matters buzzed through the air among the people on the lawn. Ocher khaddar jibbas, veshtis with soiled borders, and shawls with obscenely bright green borders—all markers of various political affiliations—could be spotted all over the place. Things got really loud when a discussion turned into a debate and then heated up into a fight. People moved their heads and hands vigorously, their faces contorted terribly, their eyes going red and swollen with anger, and they raised their voices to shut the opponent down, howling like tomcats in heat. It seemed a shrill voice was now the index of sound opinion. And local expressions had vanished without a trace! Did they know they were simply mouthing the language of newspaper headlines? When an old woman came by to sell peanuts, one of the men told her he couldn't buy any because his "budget was tight." And she took it as a perfectly acceptable response and walked away.

In the park, the evening editions of the dailies sold out in a flash. They explained the state of the times in both text and pictures. News of "runaway wives" commanded front-page headlines in big, bold letters, making men wonder if they could reasonably expect their wives to be there when they returned home. Those who managed to memorize the news acquired special prestige among friends. They were like newsreels on legs. Once these news hoarders became beacons of wisdom, they had to work hard to keep their reputation. So they tired themselves out, running to every free reading room in the area and cramming as much as they could into their heads. They no longer had the time even to stop and look at a drongo bird for a minute, or to lose themselves in the gentle flow of the river, or to walk by the shore looking for seashells.

A professor walked into the park, clad in a long-sleeved jibba and a stole draped around his neck that reached down to his knees. He had a stately bearing, his face mature beyond his years and hence smug, and eyes that surveyed all that they saw. The moment they saw him, the students sitting around smoking cigarettes on the lawn jumped up in unison and hid their cigarettes behind their backs in one quick, uniform motion. They lowered their chins and tried to blow out smoke from their mouths in little wisps, trying to making it look like they were blowing to cool off sweat. "Good evening, sir!" they said. The professor looked pleased. Like a table fan turning, he moved his head in two semicircular arcs and said, "So you are all here on the lawn."

"Yes, sir," said the students.

"A most pleasant breeze, isn't it?" he asked.

"Yes, sir. Excellent breeze," they answered in unison.

The students feared he might start reciting some classical Tamil verse. The look on his face suggested that the thought did occur to him, but he decided otherwise. He walked away, saying, "Good, good, carry on." Perhaps his problem was just that one too many songs came to his mind at the same time.

Down! Down! protest marches kept happening. Thousands marched together, shouting "Down! Down!" in unison from the pits of their stomachs. They seemed to have resolved to attain a martyr's death after a noble display of collective blood vomiting. When those sitting on the lawn inside the park heard the protest slogans coming from the street, they ran outside to watch. The protest marches moved toward available vacant plots, and onlookers rushed to find good spots. In those days of high living costs, this was the only free entertainment available, and listening to a good speech was as satisfying as a full concert by a senior musician. Since they had been doing these speeches for a hundred years or so now, they had really mastered the subtleties, much like how, after puberty, a devadasi girl came to master the nuances of her trade.

The age of the loudspeaker had dawned. Politicians, religious leaders, writers, priests, musicians, publicists—all screamed themselves hoarse into loudspeakers. Even funeral services were relayed on loudspeakers from cemeteries and burning grounds! And endless chants to Rama from the Brahmin quarters. Priests spurred on by the presence of the loudspeaker screamed into it, not bothered that their topknots had come undone in their frenzy. The unrest induced by the loudspeaker was now all-pervading.

At public meetings, both local speakers as well as out-of-towners pilloried the government mercilessly. Sometimes, they restrained themselves and stopped with cautionary remarks. Sometimes, they ridiculed the government. At other times, they started crying. When people were already assailed by miseries, here was the government trying to provoke them with yet another disastrous scheme of some kind. Now they really lost it. Choking with anguish, they unleashed their emotions and spat out blood-soaked words at the government. When they cried out, "Mr. Nehru!" raising their arms in front of them like Jesus, the force of that appeal and sentiment convinced everyone that the great Mr. Nehru was present in the room, standing right next to them. And they reasoned: it was true that Gandhiji had been assassinated, but did that mean the injustices he enabled had died with him too? So sometimes the speakers resorted to attacking Gandhiji as well, addressing him as if he were present: "This is the result of your words . . . This is the result of your actions . . ." Their staunch humanism refused to let them hold anything sacred or above criticism. Sometimes, the passion born of their righteous anger made them resort to vulgarisms, for which they apologized to the esteemed gathering, but then they went right ahead with even more obscene language.

Their mental exhaustion from carrying around their virtues for so long—and for others' sakes—had made them so wound up, they were terrified their taut nerves would shatter any minute. They dreamed about the sum of the pleasures they had given up for the sake of virtue and out of their desire for respect and regard; now, it made them wallow in self-pity. All those sacrifices they made to the dictates of their conscience seemed meaningless to them. An honorable man today felt nothing but utter contempt for his own posturing and lofty ways. He wanted to roll naked on the grassy ground in the park. He wanted to go to the nightclub and dance with the women who gyrated their hips and shook their buttocks. He wanted to stand at the street corner and shout, "I am no saint! I am just an ordinary man!" and tear off his mantle so he might plunge himself into an ocean of pleasures.

Even as we internalized herd mentality and mocked everything as phony, we were also entranced by that very phoniness. In the same way, it was also true that when we frowned at teenage girls when they abandoned their natural gait and instead took on a new fancy one, we were, in fact, also enjoying it at the same time. We had become far too cowardly to admit that nature was not all that appealing after all. When women laughed after having unlearned their own laugh, when they moved their hands or their neck after unlearning their own gestures, when they sang in a voice that was not their own, it was, in fact, quite enchanting, wasn't it? Wasn't it true that any man or woman could only hope to secure the joy of being desired by others if they resorted to such borrowings? Perhaps in the past, the face was more beautiful than the mask. But we knew nothing about those days.

How unfortunate that a person today found it impossible to discern who exactly these times required them to become! We still could not figure out which of the divine commandments we must violate. Conscience was becoming increasingly obsolete. While we heard constantly about the Gita and the Tirukkural, it seemed that the secret to the success of those who carried these texts around in their hands lay precisely in the fact that they knew when to violate them discreetly. They were in the grips of the fear that they would be ruined if they shut their eyes and obeyed anything with total and complete faith. How could ordinary people be saved by creeds that were not foolproof? Such creeds might be good enough for saints, but then saints had no need for creeds in the first place. It was also not clear how anyone could trust anything without guarantees. It had been ages since it was decreed that we must speak the truth, but we had still not determined in what circumstances we were allowed to lie. We needed to know urgently when it was acceptable to cheat someone and when, even if only as an exception to the rule, it was permissible to covet another man's wife. It seemed we could no longer bear the torments of the conscience that we could neither follow nor violate without compunction.

An international organization had built a children's playground within the park. Children could play on the slide and the seesaw, they could swing on the trapeze rings, they could turn somersaults. They came to play here in the evenings. By the time children from the convent school went home, had coffee and snacks, changed into their play clothes, and headed to the park carrying chocolates to munch later, the poor kids from the east side of town occupied everything in the playground. Now, the fathers of some of the convent-school kids were members of that international organization. So the convent kids were livid at the other kids who wouldn't even let them enjoy the things they believed were rightfully theirs. Daweed, the playground attendant, shared their feelings, but there was nothing much he could do. Once, when he attempted to expel the east-side street kids on the charge that they were damaging the facilities in the playground—which was only half true—a crowd rushed from the lawn and conducted a heated public meeting. Daweed was lucky to escape without a beating that day.

After this incident, since many advocated a compromise, they came up with a solution: the queue system. Children now queued up in front of the slide, the seesaw, and the trapeze rings. There was also a rule that children from the east side should not jump over the compound wall before the playground opened. When the gate was opened at four thirty, children entered, pushing and shoving each other to get ahead in the queue. Since the queue system did not entertain differences and disparities between boys and girls, dark-skinned and light-skinned, tall and short, local and visiting, convent-schooled and tinnai-schooled, things often went smoothly. However, the seesaw often got stalled by ill-matched pairs. When the end of the seesaw with a plump kid refused

58

to lift off the ground, the puny one at the other looked on in panic from above. There were kids in the queue who could be good matches for the two stranded children, but the system could only honor the order in which children showed up—it could not entertain any other considerations. So when more such ill-matched pairs showed up, there was an impasse, both with the seesaw as well as with the pleasure of play. Nevertheless, the system could not be changed for this. Any system has its flaws.

When children stood in the queue for a long time, it was natural for them to get tired. Eager for a chance to play on the slide and to swing from the trapeze rings, these kids stood in line until their feet hurt. They kept shifting their weight from one foot to the other. When a boy grew impatient, he looked around, and if he saw a shorter line nearby, he jumped to it. Other kids followed right on his heels. Now that everybody had moved away, they realized that the new line they had joined was now longer than the one they had been standing in, so they rushed back. All this jumping back and forth between lines felt as fun and as tiring as the slide and the see-saw. So, treating it as a game in its own right, they kept at it. Then they grew exhausted and would stop and stand wherever they were. When it grew dark, children toward the end of the line gave up and went home. As they walked away disappointed, they told themselves they wouldn't be coming back to the playground. But by the next evening, their desire to play would overcome their frustration, and they would be back at the playground. They came running as fast as they could, determined to get ahead in the line. And they stood in line for a long time.

They teared up when they thought of their plight. Whenever the attendant Daweed walked away to pee or to smoke a beedi, they all cursed him unanimously. They blamed him for everything.

X

It is quite evident that times have changed a great deal. Those days when the casuarina grove transformed into the park made me feel as if the world was spinning at a greater speed—indeed, spinning out of control. When I think back on it now, it all feels like a dream. But it also feels real.

It is going to be difficult to talk of the events that happened next; describing a tale of devastation in the minutest detail, especially of the tamarind tree, is not a pleasant task. But I have already started, and so I must go on.

5.

If a newcomer walked a mile or so past Joseph's laundry on Asaripallam Road and arrived at the majestic gateway to Ranithottam, he might think that the road ended there. If he had planned to proceed straight ahead, on the northern side, he might see a huge granite wall next to the wide entrance to Ranithottam. This wall resembled a steep hill on which giant children had traced playful designs. Right next to the entrance, on its southern side, was a massive tree, and then more trees. Perplexed that the road had suddenly ended, the newcomer might notice a bus driving past him. When the bus neared the granite wall, the newcomer would be stunned to see that, instead of crashing into the granite wall, it seemed to vanish.

This was because the turn was L-shaped, similar to the angle between the neck and the shoulder. Further ahead, the spirited newcomer might see that Asaripallam Road ran, unimpeded, a long way past Ranithottam. What hid the road from view was the canopy of the trees. Just a short way down *that* road, there was a big building opposite the grove of punnai trees. This was the bishop's palace.

If you stood on Asaripallam Road on Mondays or Thursdays at six in the morning, you would see a parade of needy children. These children had been forcibly roused from their beds and thrust out of their homes at that hour, their eyes still bleary with sleep. Torn shirts, torn sweaters, waterproof and fireproof skirts, plaited hair, lice, lesions, boils . . . Some of the kids shunned their underwear in favor of their fathers' long shirts. Others didn't find it necessary to wear shirts at all when they abandoned their underwear.

Even the tiniest of these kids would be lugging a large container; there was likely no bigger pot in their household. For two years now, the bishop had been distributing milk to children. Initially, only children from Christian families showed up; other families were afraid it might be a ruse for conversion. They might be poor, but that didn't mean they would sell their religion for some powdered milk. But after a while, when they saw how hale and healthy the Christian children looked, the Hindus too started sending their kids.

The number of kids standing outside the bishop's palace with pots and containers was enough to fill two elementary schools. The bishop saw to it that the children did not leave with empty pots or empty stomachs. Five or so stone basins as large as baby elephants were set up on the palace grounds in front of the Virgin Mary. Each time the basin was filled, the milk sloshed about in waves. If Mahavishnu could see this, he would surely give up his abode in the Ocean of Milk and move here!

When the clock struck seven, a massive crowd of children gathered in front of the bishop's palace. Children sat in the dust on either side of the road. Some of the kids peered through the gaps in the gate. One child—clad in nothing but a loincloth—was lying on his belly in front of the gate and providing a running commentary, all the while kicking himself on his bum with his heels.

"Now they are breaking open the milk-powder boxes . . . They are pouring in water . . . Hey! Don't dilute it so much . . . What are you doing, you are just pouring it in . . . There comes the bishop . . . Sir, good morning . . . Now the bearded fellow is coming to open the door . . . Be ready, everybody . . ."

This was the usual ritual. One Thursday, however, things went slightly differently. There was a sudden downpour the evening before, and the rain kept up its whimpering all night. Then, at dawn on Thursday morning, it began to pour again. The children waited at home until the rain let up a little, then ran toward the palace. A group of kids from Mada Street reached the tamarind-tree junction; they came stomping on the puddles of rainwater that had filled up the potholes in the cement road. The rain picked up again by the time they reached the tamarind tree, so they stopped under its shelter.

Rainwater dripped from the tree continuously. Those kids who were wearing shirts pulled their collars over their heads and stood, hugging their arms to their chests. Other kids wore pots and containers as helmets over their heads. Rainwater from the leaves splashed against these pots.

The rain began to subside. Just as the children were about to head out, groups of manual scavengers began to arrive under the tree—people decreed by their low caste status to be sanitation workers who did the work others didn't want to do. There were at least forty or fifty of them. Behind these groups came a man on a bicycle. He leaned his bicycle against the locked doorway of a store, opened a notebook, and started calling out names. And when they heard their name, the manual scavengers responded: "Present, present."

There was a water pump at the junction, right next to the wall around the park. One of the manual scavengers, a woman, was sitting there, totally indifferent to the dampness around the pump. Considering her age and chubbiness, there was no reason for her not to be wearing a blouse. Some of the children moved closer to her and stood, looking alternately at her and the man taking roll call. Her gaze, however, was totally focused on the tamarind tree.

"So many pods on that tree!" said the woman.

"Yes! Look at them hanging," said a little boy standing next to her. Right away, his mouth started to water. He looked around to see if anybody had noticed before swallowing his saliva.

Just then, a gust of wind shook the tree, bringing down a shower of raindrops. A tamarind pod fell in front of the woman. That little boy bent down quickly and snatched it away. Just as he raised the pod to his mouth, the woman said, "Give me half, my dear. Be a darling, please."

After a moment's hesitation, the boy broke a little piece off and offered it to her. She stuck out her tongue and rubbed the fruit against it. At that moment, her cheeks trembled and her eyes rolled back. The boys laughed at the sight, and she laughed with them.

A younger woman, also a manual scavenger, arrived at the water pump. She was quite a shapely woman. The short-sleeved checkered shirt she was wearing over her sari really brought out her figure. And her hair was not unkempt. She had oiled and combed it neatly. She wore a stack of bangles on her right arm. She had the glow of a newlywed.

She asked the other woman sitting by the pump, "Did you get nauseous and throw up today?"

"Oh my God, I threw up so much! From the moment I woke up, I felt sick in the stomach," she said, rubbing the fruit against her tongue.

The younger worker looked with some interest at the way the woman savored the tamarind fruit.

"Is it really sour?" she then asked.

"Oh yes! It is really, really is. It hits you right in the brain. Very comforting when you are feeling queasy," she said, rubbing the fruit against her tongue a few more times.

The younger woman walked over to a group of male workers. In the middle of the crowd stood a young, well-built man wearing a khaki shirt. She went up to him, tapped his shoulder, and whispered something to him while pointing at the tree. He stepped away from the crowd, and she followed him.

The roll call was over. After giving the workers instructions, the municipal worker got on his bicycle and pedaled away. The shops had not opened for business yet. The weather must have kept the shopkeepers from getting to the market on time. Since it was still drizzling nonstop, there were generally very few people out and about.

The young man looked cautiously in either direction. Next to the water pump lay a pile of stones meant to be used for road repair. He picked up a stone from that pile, took aim with his left forefinger, and threw it at the tree. A dozen or so tamarind pods showered down. The children and the younger women workers rushed to pick them up. There were no pods left for the women who came after them. Now these women went to their husbands and made sweet entreaties. More of the men stepped forward to aim stones at the tree.

Until then, the children had refrained from aiming stones at the tree because they were afraid the manual scavengers might object and pick a fight. But now they joined in with abandon. The men and the big children threw stones at the tree, while the women workers and the skinny kids gathered the pods that fell. A new group of children arrived just then from Vadiveeswaram; they joined in the fun. The manual scavengers who had been standing off to the side also joined in. Tamarind fruits came showering down. Everyone gathered as much as they could hold. The children stuffed the fruits into their milk pots. The pile of stones by the wall had vanished without a trace. And the junction lay strewn with leaves, twigs, and stones.

"Police!" a mischievous boy shouted when they were least expecting it. The children scattered away, yelling, "Long live Mahatma Gandhi!" They ran two furlongs before they realized it was a hoax.

The troop of children reached the bishop's palace an hour late that day.

The worker who was assigned to sweep under the tamarind tree did his work with extra care that Thursday. He swept most thoroughly. He even picked the stones up and piled them against the wall. When he found a national flag that had fallen down from one of the tree's branches, he rolled it up and tucked it into his veshti, thinking it would be perfect for a shirt for the new baby.

When the overseer showed up, there was not a single pod or leaf or twig lying on the ground. He could not help but mentally praise the worker who had done such a thorough job. There were still workers left who took pride in their work!

6.

The tamarind tree was the property of the town council, which owned thousands of trees around the area—scores of tamarind, mango, and neem trees. It owned more banyan trees than you could count. Wherever you turned, you found banyan trees nodding in the wind, their wide arms pointing to the sky and their aerial roots exploring the dusty earth, standing on either side of the road like large merry-go-rounds with green cymbals hanging from their rims.

Since all trees belonged to the municipality, legally speaking, all income from them belonged to the municipality too. But in reality, the municipality did not get much income from any of the trees. Everyone in town who raised goats relied entirely on the banyan trees for fodder. This, in their opinion, was the most appealing *and* most profitable aspect of raising goats: they could nourish the goats on the municipality's banyan leaves, but keep the milk for themselves.

If there was ever an exception to this state of affairs, it was the tamarind tree.

The municipality made handsome profit from the tamarind tree because of one simple reason. The tree stood at a busy junction that knew neither day nor night. Even when other parts of town went to sleep, this place was wide awake. The spot under the tree was the waiting place for people traveling out of town and people who were in transit, waiting to continue their journey back home after their visit to the seashore in Kanyakumari. It was also the spot where jugglers chose to show off their dazzling skills when they arrived in town with their wives and children. It was where the magician set up shop, beginning his act with a few magic tricks and wrapping it up by selling miraculous cures, without anyone realizing the gambit. This was where they staged ferocious fights between the mongoose and the cobra. It was also the venue for special discounted sales: everything for two and a half annas!

As if this were not crowd enough, there was also the movie theater right across the road. People headed for the first show; people who couldn't get tickets for the first show and stood by, looking bereft and lost; those who could not afford to go to the movies but who could entertain themselves by looking at the posters, catching the stray bits of background music, dialogue, and songs that reached their ears, recalling with pleasure the scenes they had watched before . . . So the place was indeed very crowded.

The crowd did not let up even at ten at night. The buses heading east began running at two thirty in the morning. At least a quarter of the people who went to the theater for the second show had to catch these buses later. They paid four annas for the pleasure of dozing off under the ceiling fans in the fancy theater, waking up now and then to catch a glimpse of women dancing onscreen, or a few fine moves of a sword fight, or a love duet. Only those who have experienced this pleasure know its value.

Amid such constant commotion, it was nearly impossible for anyone to steal tamarind pods from the tree. Even though almost everyone felt this urge at one time or another, it was still not the sort of the thing they could bring themselves to do with others watching. So it was no surprise that no fruit from that tree ever got stolen.

It was a fine tree. Year after year, it brought in an outstanding harvest. I don't know if the tree ever realized that no individual would ever make special claims on it. But I suspect it knew. No one thought of the tree as their own, but the tree seemed to exude the conviction that it belonged to everyone. Still, since the municipality owned the tamarind tree, it had rightful claim to the income from the tree. But the municipality had no use for the tamarind harvest, just as it had no use for rice or salt or black gram dal. All it needed was money—money to protect its people, take care of them, improve their lot.

Therefore, every year, the municipality auctioned away the tree for a year's lease, keeping only the cash proceeds as income.

It was a Thursday. The town crier's drum could be heard in the bazaar, announcing that the next day, at three in the afternoon, the tamarind tree would be put up for auction. And so, on Friday afternoon, a municipal employee and a helper set out from their office toward the tamarind-tree junction.

The employee's name was Vallinayagam Pillai, usually called Valli. He had been working for the municipal council for nineteen years, drawing a salary of thirty-three and a half rupees, dearness allowance included. Even though he was an ordinary employee, he wielded a great deal of influence in the office. This was because he was the only one in the entire office who was well-versed in municipal codes and procedures. He was the one who advised the mayor on how to catch a tax evader. In the same breath, he would run to said tax evader and advise him on how to dodge the consequences. The former ensured his monthly salary; the latter covered the monthly shortages. The fact that he attended to both these jobs at once ensured his family's subsistence.

Valli had a fine rosy complexion. Even though it had dulled somewhat over the years from being out in the sun, he still had his glow. Thick, combed hair. Collarless shirt. Rubber-tire-soled sandals that looked like small rafts when he took them off. The pockmarks on his face were ten years old, but they looked so fresh and deep that you would think the pox goddess had just recently blessed him.

Since they had announced the auction was at three in the afternoon, people could reasonably expect it to start only at four. Accordingly, Valli hurried to make it to the junction by four thirty. It was four fifty when he finally arrived, however. His helper placed the stool he had carried under the tamarind tree. Valli sat. He looked around. There were some scattered crowds, but no one seemed to be the type to bid in an auction. This auction had been happening every year for eleven years, and a paltry gathering like this had never been seen before. In the past years, the vendors used to throng to watch the auction! And where was that special reporter from the *Travancore Nesan* who covered the event every year without fail, writing about it in great detail and with some creative liberties?

Valli had been in charge of the auction every year, so he knew everyone who showed up. Now, in the relatively empty tamarind tree-junction, he reminisced about some of the most dramatic moments from last year . . .

⋊

The most important bidders who came to the auction every year were Vadaseri Brammananda Moopanar, Kottary Abdul Ali Sahib, and Keezhatteru Aiyamperumal Konar. If he wasn't at the maharaja's palace in Thiruvananthapuram, Thazhakudy Moothapillai would definitely come to the auction as well.

Moothapillai's arrival usually stirred a notable excitement among the crowd. The bidding wars between him and Abdul Ali Sahib were legendary, and all the vendors in the bazaar would crowd around to witness it.

Usually, Moothapillai arrived from Thazhakudy in a cart drawn by two bullocks. He was from a long line of rich landowners. He even leased the lands that belonged to the king and the temple at Vadaseri. As a result, he wielded an enormous influence in our town. He was very simple in his appearance, since he relished his reputation for simplicity. He only wore a freshly laundered, single-layered veshti. On his shoulders, a thin Vadaseri towel, also freshly laundered. And, to wipe his nose after a pinch of snuff, a black handkerchief kept at the ready at his waist.

Moothapillai had developed a persistent case of eczema on both his legs, and he hated it when the ointment rubbed off on the edge of the veshti and became coated with dust from the streets. So he always folded up his dhoti and held it well above his knees.

In past years, on the day of the auction, Moothapillai set out from his place at two in the afternoon. First, he stopped at Kottaru to buy cattle feed, special sesame-seed cakes, and a pound of fine Jaffna tobacco for himself and his wife. Then he headed straight to the tamarind-tree junction. His carriage circled the tamarind tree two or three times, with Moothapillai lying flat on his back with his head hanging outside the carriage cabin, gazing up at the tree. That was all the time he needed to assess the harvest in financial terms and to make an estimate.

During the auction, Nagaru Pillai, Moothapillai's coachman, would park the carriage across the road from the tree, in front of Abdul Khader's store. Moothapillai was always the last one to open his mouth. Until then, Nagaru Pillai would make the bids, guided by meaningful glances from his boss sitting inside the carriage.

The rule of the auction was that every successive bid had to be at least one chakram higher than the previous bid.

At the start of an auction last year, Abdul Ali Sahib and Moothapillai kept quiet, letting the others amuse themselves with their paltry bids. The year before that, the tree had gone for thirty-three rupees, and here were these novices, starting their bids around seven or seven and a half rupees! As these voices went back and forth with their silly bids, Sahib casually said, "Twenty-one rupees," looking around him as if he'd just woken up from a deep sleep. This was the point at which Moothapillai sat up straighter in his carriage. His coachman quickly glanced inside, and then shouted, "Twenty-one rupees and one chakram."

When they heard this, some of the young men in the crowd started laughing. Moothapillai always offered only one chakram more than the previous bidder. He did so because he knew that was the minimum he had to bid, according to the auction rules. His desire was to end all transactions with maximum profit or minimum loss. But these rookies did not understand that. They grinned as if they had seen someone dancing naked. But the old-timers in the crowd commended Pillai's principle. "You can't beat him! My God, he is a shark!" they said.

At this point, Brammananda Moopanar chimed in hesitatingly, "Twenty-two rupees." But Moothapillai would not respond to that. He'd open his mouth only after Sahib's bids.

"Twenty-seven rupees." This was Sahib calling out.

"Twenty-seven rupees, going once . . . going twice . . . going twice . . ." Valli's helper dragged it out.

Now Nagaru Pillai turned to look inside the carriage.

"Was that Sahib?" Moothapillai asked him.

"Yes."

"The rascal won't give up," Moothapillai grumbled, and signaled to the coachman with his index finger.

Immediately, Nagaru Pillai shouted, "Twenty-seven rupees and one chakram."

The crowd erupted in laughter again.

"Twenty-seven rupees and two chakram!" someone teased.

Laughter again in the crowd.

Moothapillai was not offended by any of this. He assumed that the crowd was in fact laughing at Sahib's hasty bids.

"Going once . . . going twice . . . going twice . . ."

Sahib was beginning to feel angry. "Thirty-two rupees," he struck back, a little too loudly. The crowd was stunned. A dozen or so bidders backed out.

This was the most crucial moment. At this point, Sahib's bid had come close to the previous year's price. Everyone looked toward the carriage, eager to see what Moothapillai's driver would bid next. But what emerged from the carriage were two eczema-afflicted legs and a walking stick. Nagaru Pillai jumped from the front of the carriage and came to Moothapillai's assistance.

Holding his doubled-up veshti in his left hand and leaning on Nagaru Pillai's arm, Moothapillai crossed the cement road and walked toward the tamarind tree. At Valli's insistence, he took a seat at the stool. He raised his head and studied the tamarind tree carefully. A snicker rippled through the crowd. Sahib looked around at everyone in smug satisfaction. He only needed one look at the tree to make his decision; he wouldn't be caught dead looking at it again.

"Son-in-law, tell me, who made the last bid? How much was it?" Moothapillai asked Valli.

Municipal employee Valli's first wife was Thazhakudy Moothapillai's neighbor Aachi's cousin's sister's daughter. The crowd had no way of knowing this connection. Now, after hearing Moothapillai's address of endearment to Valli, they couldn't help but wonder how close these two were.

"It was Sahib who bid last," Valli replied. "Thirty-two rupees."

"Is that so? Why not? He makes money every time the sun shines," said Moothapillai.

People laughed with great delight at the joke. Many in the crowd knew that Sahib owned several salt pans.

The helper raised his voice again. "Going once . . . going twice . . . going twice . . ."

Moothapillai said calmly, "Thirty-two rupees and one chakram."

The youngsters roared with laughter. The older folks still said, "My God! You can't beat him, can you?" But there was no change in Moothapillai's facial expression. He sat there still like the main deity in a temple.

⋈

Today, the day of the auction this year, Valli just stood there, reminiscing about past years and chuckling to himself.

73

Moothapillai was nowhere to be seen. Where was Sahib? And Konar only lived a stone's throw away. What had happened to him too? And whatever had happened to the crowds that used to gather to watch the fun?

Just then he heard someone address him: "*Annachi*, brother, can you come here, please?" He turned to see Dhamu standing inside his shop and signaling to him. Dhamu was a shopkeeper who owned the general store right under the tamarind tree, opposite Abdul Khader's famous stationery shop.

Slowly Valli walked over to the shop. His helper walked behind him, carrying the stool. The coolie, Ayyappan, was standing at the shop as well, his left hand over some soda bottles stacked up to one side and his right hand over his mouth, hiding his laughter.

"What brings you here, *annachi*?" Dhamu asked.

Valli was distracted by coolie Ayyappan, who had turned his face away toward the store and was howling with laughter. What was up with him? Focusing on Dhamu again, Valli said: "I am here for the auction?"

"Ah, the auction," Dhamu said. "How much do you think it will fetch this time?"

"Forty-five rupees, by my estimate."

"What? The price has gone up?"

"Yes! Excellent harvest this year, isn't it?"

At this point, coolie Ayyappan doubled over with laughter and quickly slipped out of sight. They heard him bursting with laughter. "*Dei!* What's so funny? Is someone dancing naked over here?" Valli shouted at him in anger. His hand still covering his mouth, Ayyappan ran toward the entrance to the municipal park. Valli grew red with rage.

"*Annachi*, don't be angry," said Dhamu.

"No. I have been watching him for a while now. He has a stupid grin all the time. Every time I look at his face, I feel like slapping him. One of these days I am going to catch hold of him. Then he will know. Idiot!"

"You can yell at him later. Look at the tree first," Dhamu said.

Before Valli could look, his helper gasped: "There is not a single pod on the tree!"

Valli simply stared at the tree. "What happened to all the tamarind pods?" he asked quietly.

Dhamu didn't answer.

"I am asking you, what happened to all the pods on the tree?"

"Well, there is a police station just two furlongs from here," Dhamu said, with a look of indifference.

"Dhamu, I know you very well."

"*Annachi*, I know you too."

"Fine. We'll see."

"We'll see."

Valli stormed off.

"I saw him standing around, looking confused. So I called him over to let him know. And he attacks me!" Dhamu said to the customer who came for some betel.

As Valli and the helper passed the clock tower, they heard someone clapping their hands and calling out to them, so they turned to see who it was. There, in front of Lala Sweet Shop, stood Moopanar and Sahib, the latter wearing a towel so long it grazed the ground, a tamarind-leaf design on its border. Valli panicked. "Just keep walking behind me. Don't look back," he ordered his helper, and they quickened their pace.

They managed to escape Moopanar and Sahib, but just as they were passing Ananda Bhavan Hotel, they heard someone else shout, "Son-in-law, over here!" It was Moothapillai, sitting in his carriage. He was holding a tumbler in his right hand; Nagaru Pillai was standing outside the carriage and pouring coffee from a bowl into the tumbler.

There was no escape.

"*Annachi,*" greeted Valli.

"How much did the tree go for?" Moothapillai asked, his eyes fixed on the coffee in his tumbler.

"You didn't come!"

"Why should I go to the auction and keep fighting with Sahib year after year? I saw him going just now. He walks with his nose in the air, his towel sweeping the ground. He thinks he will make a lakh from this. Let him! What do you say?"

"Sounds right."

"So," Moothapillai asked again, "how much did it go for?"

"The auction didn't happen. There was a small complication."

"What complication?"

"There were no pods."

"On the tree?"

"Yes."

"Not even one?"

"Not even one."

"Then there is no complication. There were no pods, there was no auction. Why do you call it a complication?"

"That's right, that's right."

"Theft?"

"I don't know."

"It can't be theft," Moothapillai said. "Maybe sparrows ate them?"

At this point, Moothapillai exchanged a quick glance with Nagaru Pillai and winked.

"Then they would have eaten them every year, wouldn't they?" asked Valli.

"But there are a lot more sparrows this year, you know."

"Why is that?"

"Who knows why? Sparrows, grasshoppers, rats, bandicoots, lizards, mosquitoes, there is more of everything this year. Aren't we in August already? But we have still not had a drop of rain, have we?"

Valli contemplated this. "Why do you think that is?"

"Because earlier, there was one man ruling the kingdom. Now there are ten men running things."

"Oh! You are talking about that!"

"What am I talking about? See, in a kingdom, there should be one man issuing commands and others obeying," Moothapillai said, warming up to his favorite subject. "But what is happening now is sheer madness. Take my home for example. If I, my wife, my children, my driver, my maid, my servant, everyone gets to have a say in how things are run, then who is going to do the bidding? Do you understand what I mean?"

"I do."

"Oh, here comes all the maharajas!"

Valli turned. A crowd was approaching, with Sahib and Moopanar in the lead. Valli's eyes widened. "*Annachi*, I will take leave. I need to go write up the report," he said, walking away in a hurry. "Hey! Hey!" Sahib called out, clapping his hands. Moopanar was clapping his hands too. Valli walked as fast as he could, waving his left hand behind him in a hurried goodbye.

"Running away in humiliation!" said Moothapillai, shaking with laughter. "Serves them right for coveting what belongs to our Lord Padmanabha!" He laughed even harder, Nagaru Pillai joining in. When Sahib and Moopanar reached the carriage, the three bidders fell into a discussion about the current fate of the tamarind tree. A crowd gathered around them, joining the speculation.

"Was it theft?" asked Moothapillai.

"I have no idea," said Sahib.

"I came by around two o'clock to take a look," Moothapillai said. "There was not a single pod on the tree. So I went away to Kambolam."

"So then it was definitely theft?" asked the elderly man standing behind Sahib. He was wearing an open coat and canvas shoes.

"Mark my words. From now on, this is exactly how things are going to be run in this country. Even the Chokkans and Sudalais of the world are now up in arms to rule the country, aren't they? As far as I know, the auction has gone on for decades now. Some twenty or twenty-five years ago, it was only two and a half rupees. Yes, that's right—nine chakrams. I have won the bid myself several times. This is the first time the auction has fallen through. But this is just the beginning, let me tell you. Soon someone will strip the veshti off your waist even as you are walking down the road. Ask why, and he will say, 'This is just my second veshti. Anyway, I can see that you are wearing a loincloth. So you are fine.' Even if a crowd gathers at the scene, they will all support him."

Everyone standing in front of the carriage erupted in laughter. "Well put!" said the elderly man. Someone else in the crowd asked: "Moothapillai, have you been to the palace of late?"

"Yes. About this time last week I was there, speaking to His Highness. He made me sit with him as an equal and talked to me for a long time."

"Is he in low spirits?"

"Low spirits? Of course he is in low spirits! What do you expect? We lose a bit of harvest in an auction, and we bawl and scream and carry on like anything. Here an entire kingdom has slipped through his fingers. That must surely hurt a lot. He told me he asked them to go ahead and take it. 'Take it . . . govern it well . . . treat my people with respect . . . honor Lord Padmanabha.' He still has his title and status. His possessions, palace, money, staff, driver, maid. He gets to keep them all. And the annual anointing ceremony will happen as usual. But nevertheless, he is feeling down."

"If he asks for the kingdom back, will they oblige?" the old man in the open coat asked.

The crowd burst into laughter and sniggers. Moothapillai surveyed their faces and realized there were a lot of young men standing there, boys who wouldn't know anything of the old times. "I am going to the municipal office to file a complaint. Anyone who wants to join me can come with me. Nagaru, let's go."

Moothapillai's carriage set off toward the municipal office. About fifty people followed him.

7.

About half a mile to the north of the tamarind-tree junction, if you turned left and walked past St. Joseph's College and the Kallar pond, you would see the Sri Lankan Pentecostal Mission's building with its four-foot-high compound wall. The road climbs steeply at this point, rising up to the height of a palm tree in less than an eighth of a mile. At its highest point, just before the road starts coming down again, there is a narrow lane that branches off to the left, running straight as a warp of looms on the weavers' street before it vanishes under a green gate. That's the path to the municipal office.

The raddled building behind the green gate, the one that looks like a deranged holy man, is the municipal office building. It once used to belong to Muhaideen Bacha Sahib, who was a close friend of Damodara Asan. In those days, Bacha Sahib housed a few of his wives in this building. The legend was that he employed five or six eunuchs to guard the harem and to do odd jobs around the property. I even heard that one of the eunuchs committed suicide. During Bacha Sahib's last days, when he lay dying of advanced leprosy in the hospital, this building came up for auction, and the municipality bought it for seventy-three thousand. Even back then, give or take, it was easily worth ninety thousand. But who had that kind of money in those days? It was hard to sell even three sacks of rice for more than three or three and half rupees.

It was in the shed behind this building, which once used to be a stable for Bacha Sahib's horses, where the municipal council now held its meetings. But there was no need to look down upon it simply because it used to be a stable. After the municipality took over, it got a new roof thatched with palm planks and had its walls plastered and whitewashed.

Now, on the fateful day of the failed tamarind-tree auction, Valli opened the gate and entered the premises. His helper followed him before turning around to latch the gate. Startled, he shouted: "There's a big crowd headed this way!"

Valli turned around to look. There was a bullock cart in front and a crowd behind it, all crawling toward the municipal office. Since the crowd had to squeeze itself into the narrow lane, it was stretched out long and appeared to be bigger than it actually was. The scene petrified Valli. He rushed anxiously into the building and climbed the stairs two at a time, his rubber-soled sandals making a flapping noise as he strode past a row of clerks without so much as a glance toward them. Pushing open the half doors to the municipal commissioner's office, he burst in. The big chair on the other side of the desk was empty. The peon was dusting files and tying them up in bundles.

"Where's sir?" Valli asked him.

The peon went to the window, draped himself over it to hang his head outside, spat out a stream of betel juice, and then asked, "What's the matter, *annachi*?"

"This is urgent. Just tell me where he is."

"The council is in session, don't you remember?" The peon held out his left hand toward Valli. "Give me a bit of snuff, brother!" Valli turned and stormed back down the stairs. The peon trailed after him. "Brother, come on, give me some snuff before you go," he implored. "What's the matter? At least tell me that."

"The tamarind tree has been robbed. Not a single pod left," Valli said without breaking his stride.

"So what?" the peon said, flicking his right hand in a gesture of dismissal. "Why get so agitated for that?" Losing interest, he walked back to the office.

Things were in a state of uproar in the shed. The council session was in full swing. Valli was quite accustomed to the noise. He entered the shed, walked right up to the chairman, M. C. Joseph, and stood next to his chair. Noticing the expression on Valli's face, the chairman frowned.

"Something urgent," Valli whispered in his ear.

"Tell me."

Valli hesitated. He shot a quick glance outside the shed and then looked at the chairman again.

The chairman smiled pleasantly at the council members before him and quietly walked outside, keeping his head down. Outside the shed, he paused, holding a bamboo pipe that jutted from the slanting roof of the shed, and looked at Valli. Inside the shed, the council meeting had gone absolutely quiet. Neither Valli nor the chairman had to glance inside to know that everyone was watching them. Valli had planned to disclose the matter with as little fuss as possible. He now realized that he'd failed at it at the outset.

"Get on with it, man," said the chairman.

"You know, the tamarind-tree auction was today," said Valli, measuring his words carefully. There was a childlike innocence in his face.

"How much did it go for?"

"The auction didn't happen."

"Why? No one showed up?"

"No, there weren't any pods to auction."

"No pods? What do you mean?"

"Not a single pod."

"But you filed the report last week yourself!"

"Yes."

"What do you mean 'yes'?!"

"I estimated it at forty-five rupees."

"So what the hell happened?"

"The pods were there then."

"And now?"

"Not a single one."

"Theft?"

"I don't know."

The chairman turned to look at the council, all of whom were still staring at them.

"There's something else," Valli said, his voice low. "There's a big crowd gathered outside."

Chairman M. C. Joseph did a double take. "What now?"

"A crowd. You know that Thazhakudy Moothapillai. You know what a troublesome fellow he is. He has dragged everyone here to discuss the matter."

"So now I have to go and attend to that?"

"No, you don't have to go. Quietly delegate it to somebody else."

"Who?"

"The Palm Tree."

"The tall guy from Ward Twenty-Three?"

"That's the guy. He will get things under control. If *you* go, they will blow it out of proportion."

The chairman walked back into the shed and sat in his chair. Gnanasigamani, the leader of the opposition party, stood up. "If there is something the council needs to know," he said loudly, "you should tell us." As if on cue, everyone else—Maria Anthony, Kuriakose, Anbayya, V. V. S. Pillai, Kambaramayanam Ananthan Pillai, Chellasami, V. X. Fernandez (Junior)—jumped up in unison and bellowed: *"You have to share it with the council!"*

The chairman told the council what had happened.

Umaiyorubagam Pillai stood up. "This sounds like a serious matter. We need to set up an inquiry committee." A few from the ruling party and every member of the opposition party seconded that motion. So an inquiry committee was set up. Umaiyorubagam Pillai was to head the committee. Six other members were appointed.

Then the council adjourned.

Chairman M. C. Joseph stepped outside and whispered in Kambaramayanam Ananthan Pillai's ear. This was the man from Ward 23, whom Valli had called "the Palm Tree." Kambaramayanam Ananthan Pillai listened intently. "That's it?" he said. "Don't worry. I will get rid of them. They will even applaud me and then quietly disperse like good children." He rushed toward the front of the building to take care of the crowd.

When Chairman M. C. Joseph returned to his office, Moothapillai, Sahib, and Konar were seated in a row.

"We just thought we'd talk to you in person, that's all," Sahib said, conversationally.

"Not to worry. The tamarind tree is still standing at the junction," Moothapillai joked, winking at his driver, Nagaru Pillai, who was looking in from outside.

"We have formed a committee," Chairman M. C. Joseph said quickly. "Nothing like this has ever happened before, but I will take all necessary action. Very responsible of you to come in person . . ."

"Right, right," said Moothapillai.

Outside, they could hear people shouting, *"Long live Mahatma Gandhi!"* Valli entered the office, shaking his head in amazement. "Kambaramayanam Ananthan Pillai was amazing," he said. "He delivered. The crowd dispersed, but they trashed a few plants on their way out."

"So then we will take leave," Konar said, rising and pressing his palms together respectfully.

Sahib stood up too and looked at Moothapillai, who remained seated. "You go ahead," said Moothapillai. "I will join you shortly."

Sahib walked away, muttering under his breath, "Yeah, yeah, I am sure you have things to whisper in his ears." Konar followed him.

Glancing quickly to make sure they were gone, Moothapillai thrust his body forward and pointed to the wall in front of him. "Just a small matter. There used to be a picture hanging there. What happened to it?"

"You mean the picture of our maharaja?" the chairman asked.

83

"Yes."

"We have moved it inside."

"What do you plan to do with it?"

The chairman looked over at Valli. "What are we supposed to do with it?"

"We give it a little time and then auction it," Valli said.

"That's what I hoped to hear!" Moothapillai leaned back, satisfied. "Just let me know when you plan the auction. That's all I ask. Even if it goes five or ten rupees over the asking price, I don't mind. I want to buy it."

"Oh, sure. Why not? We'll be happy to do that," said the chairman.

"Don't let it get stolen!"

The chairman made a great show of laughing at that remark. Moothapillai took his leave, making the appropriate gestures of respect. When it looked as if Valli would follow him, the chairman asked him to stay behind. "Don't worry, I'll be back in a second," Valli said, and escorted Moothapillai to his carriage. As he climbed into his carriage, Moothapillai said to Valli, "Don't forget, *thambi*. I want that photograph. It doesn't matter if it goes five or ten rupees over the asking price."

"Definitely, *annachi*," said Valli, and Moothapillai left.

X

When Valli returned to the office, the chairman asked, "So it was theft?" Valli didn't answer right away. He leaned against the wall, and it looked like he was doing some serious thinking, sweat streaming down from his ears to his neck.

As he waited for Valli to answer, Chairman M. C. Joseph removed the chain that was attached to one of his coat buttons, pulled out the pocket watch, and placed it on the table. He removed his long coat and draped it over the back of the chair. Then he loosened his four-inch-thick belt. He picked up a mirror from a table drawer, examined his face, and smoothed down his thick mustache to cover his lips. Then he parted it in the middle and stroked it down on both sides. "Hey, what the hell are you still standing for? Sit down on that stool," he commanded Valli good-naturedly.

When Valli drew the stool toward him, the chairman said, "Before you sit down, please turn on that fan."

Valli turned the fan on and sat down on the stool.

"So it was theft?"

"How can we be certain of that?" Valli said. "It might have been. We didn't see it happen."

"Do you have other suspicions? I was wondering . . . about this Gnanasigamani crowd . . ." The chairman was, of course, referring to the leader of the opposition party, Gnanasigamani, and his party members.

"Oh! You mean the guys from Mangala Street? As if they'd dare to do anything!"

"Hey! Hey! Careful what you say! I am from Mangala Street too. You hit dangerously close to home there."

Valli suddenly realized what he had said. "You might be from that street," he said, carefully, "but that does not mean you are all of a piece. People have their own personalities, don't they?"

"All right, all right, change the subject," the chairman said, straightening his collar. "What a thing to say! You got me all worked up."

Keen on changing the subject, Valli said, "My suspicions are not on the opposition party."

"Really?"

"Really."

"Then who else?"

"I have a feeling these scavenger fellows might have done it."

"Why would they want to steal the tamarind pods?"

"You take them too lightly. They might have been naive and stupid once. But these days there are men among them who want to sit in that chair of yours and put their feet up on that table. But then, why blame them? We have just handed them all the power to vote, haven't we? So of course they will be cheeky."

"Can you get to your point?"

"That's my point. These guys are now organized and unionized. They are demanding higher wages. They are asking for bonuses. They want us to build them all bungalows. They want us to buy them all gramophones. They have started making their demands. But you don't seem to relent. So they have decided to teach you a lesson . . ."

"You really think they would go to that extent?"

"Oh, the state of things today! All the big parties are behind them now. Do you know Padmanabhapuram Kodhandarama Iyer's son?"

"You mean the one with the beard."

"That's the one. Bearded. Dark. Short, stout fellow."

"Yes, yes. Janardhanan, right?"

"We used to call him Sathu. When he was little, he was like a water buffalo. The way he would splash around in the Nagaramman tank! He always muddied the water and ruined it for everyone. No one else could enjoy a decent bath. People complained to me. So one day, I took matters in my hands, and I grabbed him by the ear and dragged him out of the pond. 'How could you twist my ear?' he protested. I said to him, 'Don't waste your breath. I know you, and I also know your father.' Apparently, he went straight to his father and complained about me. You know what his father said? 'Valli from the municipality? He is close to our family! He did the right thing!' You see, Padmanabhapuram Iyer and I were classmates at the Malayalam school when we were young. In those days, Iyer used to cheat a lot in the exams. He'd copy the answers from me. 'Valli, Valli, show me the answer, come on . . . ,' he'd say, nudging me on the knee until it felt sore . . ."

"You have really gone off topic."

"I have not gone anywhere. You called his son 'Janardhanan' formally, like he is some stranger. That's why I told you that story. Even these days, when he is out somewhere, decked in his black party colors, he shouts out to me, 'Hey, Vallinayagam Pillai! It still hurts where you twisted my ear that day!'" Valli laughed, and Chairman M. C. Joseph joined in.

When the peon entered the office, Valli rose hurriedly from the stool, unwilling to be seen sitting in front of his superior. "I hear they smashed the plants on their way out. Go take care of that," the chairman said to the peon, who went back out. Valli sat down again.

"Where was I?" he asked.

"You were talking about that fellow."

"Ah yes, that's right. Him—Sathu, the one you call Janardhanan. Then he made something of himself. He studied to be a lawyer. He used to say, 'I finished my degree in a hurry and rushed back here so that I could protest and get arrested. But before I could do all that, this Gandhi had already got us our independence! He cheated me out of it.' So he hung out a sign and started a private practice as a lawyer. But no clients. He did his utmost to get some people to hire him, but nothing worked. Whenever some hapless fellow did end up hiring him as his lawyer, well, that was the end of him. If he represented the plaintiff, the defendant was sure to win. So he decided to completely change his line of work. Now he walks around with his arms around the shoulders of the manual scavengers. You should hear him talk to our Madasami. 'Comrade' this, 'Comrade' that! Like they were born from the same womb and had been close forever! Do you see what I am getting at?"

"You are suggesting he might be behind this?"

"I suspect it, yes. These fellows were quietly going about their work. But now he has changed them. They see things differently. They want benefits. They want allowances. They are demanding we set up a general store. They are asking for maternity leave. And their women? They want tassels for their broomsticks! Apparently, that will make them stylish. 'You give us just a sari and a uniform. Why not a bodice? The kind we tie at the back . . .' This is the scavenger women talking!"

"Stop it! Stop it! You've got to stop!" bellowed the chairman, waving his hand and breathless with laughter. "I get all that. But what do we do now?"

"We need to make a complaint."

"With the police?"

"Yes."

"You seem to know everything that is going on, and you still say we need to file a complaint with the police! Don't you know the police are just waiting for a chance to get one up on the municipality?!"

"I am aware of that. But I still think we need to file a police complaint."

"What the hell for?"

"What are you talking about, Chairman? How do you plan to explain this whole fiasco when they bring this up at the next council meeting?"

"Oh! So for the council . . ."

"Yes! Don't we need something to show them? We can't go tell them, 'The police are looking down at us, so we didn't file a complaint,' can we? In practice, we may deviate from official process, but the paper-work has to be in order."

"You are right, you are right," said the chairman.

"So let's file a complaint. Let the official things happen as they should."

"The police are going to be thrilled about this. They will think, *Look at these uppity fellows! They need our help now!*" The chairman paused. "Valli . . . I have a doubt. What if it was the police who . . ."

"Don't say it! It is all right to think it, but it shouldn't come from our lips!"

They heard footsteps from the veranda, and a face appeared over the half door. Business was resuming. "All right," said M. C. Joseph hurriedly to Valli. "We will talk about this later. I will send a formal complaint."

Satisfied, Valli nodded and left.

8.

Elsewhere in town, another crucial piece of the drama was unfolding.

At nine on Saturday morning, Paramarthalingam arrived at Abdul Khader's famous stationery store as usual, after collecting the keys from the owner's house. He was stunned to find shards of red glass strewn all over the entrance. He could not understand where all that glass had come from. He stood, holding his bicycle, agitated and looking around for some explanation.

Coolie Ayyappan was sitting beneath the tamarind tree and watching Paramarthalingam. Now he walked up to him and said, "*Anney,* look above you."

Paramarthalingam looked. The store sign was broken, and the wires on which the letters had been affixed were exposed. All that was left on the board was half of a letter still hanging on. "The board is broken! How did this happen?" Paramarthalingam exclaimed. Coolie Ayyappan just opened out his palms to suggest he knew nothing about it and walked away.

Paramarthalingam opened the store and made a call to Abdul Khader. The boys who worked in the store arrived one by one. They stood outside, looking alternately at the broken sign and the shards of glass on the ground. When they heard the owner's car, they rushed in and stationed themselves behind the long counters.

That sign had cost around two thousand rupees. They had placed the order with a company in Bombay, and it was not even fifteen days since the men from that company's Madras branch had installed it. In fact, no other store in the entire district had such a novel signboard. When turned on, each letter lit up in sequence. Then all the letters went off at once and the entire thing started all over, each letter lighting up one after the other. The day they had installed it, a crowd gathered in the street to watch. All the other merchants stepped outside their shops to look at it. Khader was very pleased that day. He felt as if this was the moment he was recognized as the leading merchant in the district.

Now Khader sat silently in his chair. On the table in front of him was a little nutmeg box full of red shards of glass.

Esakki came up the stairs and into the shop, saying, "Boss, ours is the only sign broken."

"What about the movie theater's sign?"

"No."

"So ours is the only store sign that's been broken?"

The boys remained silent.

All store signs stayed out in the open all the time. Nobody seemed to lock up the signs indoors when they counted the day's proceeds and secured them in the safe at closing time. It was true that during the war, light bulbs were often stolen, but that was because they were in short supply. But even that happened only in vulnerable locations and only from house verandas, bathrooms, and car sheds. Never from the bazaar. There was no way someone could stand out on the street and aim stones at a store sign with no one to witness the deed. In that entire neighborhood, the tamarind junction was the one place that was never deserted. The second show at the cinema ended only at one thirty. Until then, there was always a crowd around the tree. Moreover, buses bound for Tirunelveli left from behind the tamarind tree at four in the morning and then every forty minutes thereafter. And by six, all the small merchants arrived to open up their shops. If it was a market day, they arrived even earlier, by four in the morning, to carry their wicker baskets. Those who planned to bathe in the Pazhayar River opened their stores to take the towels they'd hung out to dry in the back. They rubbed some oil on their heads and used burnt rice husk to brush their teeth. In addition to all this commotion, there was also the private Gorkha security that the merchants paid for, and that was over and above the regular police beat.

In such a setting, how did his store sign alone come to be vandalized? The moment the store boy called him to inform him of the situation, Khader had certain suspicions. Now that he knew his store was the lone target, he had reason to believe his suspicions were correct. This was no accident; it was clearly planned. The faint sense of foreboding he had been feeling of late that something untoward was about to occur had now come to pass.

Khader called out the boys by name, one by one. They had stationed themselves behind stacks of boxes, making sure they were not in their boss's direct line of vision. Now they all stepped out, one by one, and stood next to the steel safe.

"So," Khader said. "Who did this?"

No one spoke.

"This entire time you were all whispering to one another over there. Now that I ask you to speak, you fall silent. Are you afraid that you will be called to testify in court? Out with it!"

No one responded.

But it looked like Muthu alone was murmuring something. He was hidden behind the taller, older boys. Muthu was the youngest of the lot.

"What is Muthu saying?" asked Khader.

The boys parted to give way for Muthu. Muthu continued to try to hide, but one of the boys turned around to pull him by the shoulder to push him forward.

The moment Muthu was in the front, Bacha, who was standing behind him, said: "Maybe the schoolboys broke it?"

"How could the schoolboys break it?" Khader said. "They can't be throwing stones in the junction in the middle of the day, can they?"

"No, that's not possible," said Bacha.

"It is very busy at the junction till two at night."

"That's true."

"So how could it be the schoolboys? You think they set an alarm to wake up *after* two so they could throw stones and break the sign?"

"No, you are right. It couldn't have been them."

Khader looked Muthu in the face. "What were you murmuring? Tell me."

"I was wondering if it could be some bird that broke it," Muthu replied.

All the boys broke into laughter. Muthu's face went red with embarrassment. Khader glared at the older boys. "You won't speak, but you will make fun of the one who does? Muthu, don't worry about them. Go ahead, tell me." Khader pulled Muthu by his right arm, bringing him closer.

"I was saying," said Muthu in the most tentative voice, "it could have been a kite or an eagle that broke it."

"*Dei!* Earlier you said it was a sparrow!" said Aziz from behind.

Muthu whipped his head around and shouted, "I never said it was a sparrow."

"Hey! Hey!" said Khader. "All of you, go back and stand behind your counters."

All the boys did as they were told and stood looking at Muthu.

"Hey, Muthu, why are you looking at them? Look at me and tell me. How could a kite or an eagle break the store sign?"

"So an eagle comes flying . . ." Muthu began.

"OK. It comes. Then what happens?"

"It comes and sits near the store sign."

"OK . . ."

"It is red, isn't it?"

"What is?"

"The board."

"That's right. It is bright red in color."

"So it looks like a banyan fruit, or like red banana."

"Right."

Two of the boys clamped their hands over their mouths and ran toward the back of the store; they couldn't hold their laughter.

"So you were saying the eagle might think it is a ripe fruit," Khader said. "What happens then? Why are you looking at them? Talk to me."

Muthu's face flushed red again. He started speaking fast. "So because it thinks it is a ripe red fruit, the eagle starts pecking at it. The other birds see it and think this bird has found a fruit. Then they all join together and keep pecking at it."

"There's a logic to what you are saying," said Khader.

Muthu found that encouraging. "So all the eagles broke it by pecking at it all at once," he finished.

"There is no need at all for you all to snigger," Khader shouted at the boys. "At least he has an explanation to offer. You have nothing."

After a few seconds, he addressed Muthu again.

"Listen, Muthu, an eagle has wings, doesn't it?" Khader asked.

"Yes, it does."

"How many?"

"Two."

"Fine. You say it was an eagle that broke the sign. You are right. But you see, it was actually an eagle *without* wings."

Muthu stared at Khader, his eyes wide in wonder.

"Want to see that eagle?"

Muthu nodded his head tentatively.

"All right. Go over to the storefront, go down the stairs, and stand right there."

Muthu went over to the steps.

"Go one step further down."

All the boys were looking at Khader.

"Muthu, look to the right of the tamarind tree. Hey! I said right; you are looking to the left. Ah, yes, good. Now start counting the stores one by one from there. Now look at the shops to the south. Stop at the fourth one. Do you see him? Do you see Dhamu the shopkeeper, that ugly little demon sitting there, dark and short and wearing a towel well below his navel? So much hair on his chest, like a bear? Do you see it? Don't laugh. There's your eagle. That's the eagle that broke our store sign. Dhamu didn't break it because he thought it was a fruit. No. He broke it because he is jealous. He is consumed by envy. It burns in his heart like fire. You see, this beast was not born to a mother and a father. And it grossly underestimates Khader. It is true—once upon a time, this Khader used to sit in the storefront, rolling beedis. I don't deny that. What the beast doesn't know is that I don't care if I go back to sit in the storefront, with a winnowing pan, rolling tobacco. But I won't hesitate to ruin anyone who tries to undermine me."

Paramarthalingam and Bacha came closer and said: "We had the same suspicion, boss." Bacha turned to the boys for support. "That's what we said, didn't we?"

"Yet you didn't say a word when I asked you," Khader snapped.

"How can we say something like that outright? It was just a suspicion."

"Muthu, ask the driver to bring the car around. And keep this box in the car. We're going to the police station."

9.

Khader's family was from Thakkalai. His was one of the families that had fled south during the Moplah uprising in the Malabar. His ancestors on his father's side had served the mosque for several generations. Initially, Khader's father had also been in a position of responsibility at the mosque, but in time, his piety grew so intense that he lost interest in worldly matters and started neglecting even basic religious duties, so was dismissed.

Even after being dismissed from his position at the mosque, his father spent most of his days there in meditation, and Khader remembered how, every time his annoyed mother sent him as a little boy to fetch his father at mealtimes, the man could not tear himself away from the spot.

Long after, when Khader had grown up, amassed a great deal of wealth, and earned the reputation as the leading merchant in the entire district, he still felt very emotional whenever he spoke of his childhood to his friends and invariably ended up calling his father all sorts of names. "That bastard never held me in his arms, not once!" he often said. And he laughed when he described what his mother used to call his father: "That mosque owl!" "The poor woman," he said. "She never got to enjoy life in any way. I ran away from home at eleven, because I was resolved I would make something of myself and give her all that she desired. But she died before I could make enough money."

Even at a very young age, Khader learned one of life's essential truths. He understood that the god of money was the most powerful of all gods, and that even in those aspects of life that had nothing to do with money, the power of money still prevailed. He could sense this logic, this reign of money, behind the way everyone in town laughed at his father but praised the piety of a man like P. V. Mudalali, a local businessman. But the most instructive lesson he got about the meaning of money was when he found himself infatuated with a woman at the temple float festival. The young woman's mother was all too ready to send her to his room for fifty rupees and even bolted the door on the outside. The two were out of their clothes in no time, which then lay crumpled in a corner of the room. The experience made him realize that once he had the power of money on his side, things would simply come to him, or he could always buy them for a price.

He dreamed about a bungalow, a car, a tea estate, chicken to eat every day, nothing but silk shirts to wear, a gold chain, a watch . . . He later added a beautiful woman to that list. A woman more beautiful than his mother . . . Would it come true? Why not? With Allah's grace, every desire will be fulfilled. So many beautiful women in Mekkamandapam and Thiruvithamcode . . . How often had he glimpsed their beautiful feet under door curtains, their anklets jingling with every step? If he became rich, he could have one of those women. He truly believed that it would happen one day soon.

Once he made enough money, he would send for his father or drag him over to his place. He would give the man his own private room in the bungalow and make sure he was provided with regular meals; he would allow him to spend his life meditating. He could even give his father an allowance for clothes and other odd expenses. But he could do nothing about the fact that there was no longer any relationship between his mother and father. They had nothing to say to each other. She wouldn't even look at him. And why should she? Let the father watch how the son cherished his mother and attended to her needs. It wasn't enough to marry a beautiful woman; a man should also cherish and take care of her. But how could his father's dreary mind comprehend this? Well, Khader decided that it had to be done whether or not his father could comprehend it. Even if his father didn't, surely everyone in town would understand. They would compare him to his father, and they would praise him. He wanted to hear those praises. That was what he wanted. He also wanted to be able to enjoy his wealth to the utmost but without ruining his health. He resolved that he would enjoy the women of his choice. All the pleasures that this world had to offer, or the pleasures that people said the world had to offer—he desired to experience them all and reach his own judgments about them.

It would be hard to describe the things that Khader had accomplished in the ten or fifteen years since he'd run away from home. In fact, even Khader would struggle to narrate those events in proper sequence. The way he saw it, every object, every situation, every event, every crisis—behind everything lay a way to make money. He was able to discern that possibility in anything in his very first glance, and then everything else receded from his view. This perspective then gave way to ideas, efforts, resilience in the face of failure, an agreeable manner, flexibility, and courage. He was able to approach anybody without any fear or diffidence. He was also able to forget them completely once they had served his purpose. He did not fool himself into thinking that principles were set in stone.

Later on, he delighted in telling his friends about the very first time he earned an entire rupee. While he was employed at the Noor Jahan Hotel, he ran a side hustle. He sold packets of powdered rice husk, for a paisa each, to people who brushed their teeth at the local pond, and over time he managed to make an entire rupee. Khader used to tell his friends that even when the hotel owner caught him scooping rice-husk powder into the folds of his clothes and kicked him out that day, the joy of holding a whole rupee in his hand outweighed everything else.

From the age of twelve to twenty-two, he was engaged in innumerable jobs—and what a staggering variety of jobs they were! He sold balloons and kites at the Suchindram chariot festival. He assembled picture frames at Kolappan Asari's shop. He rolled beedis. He repaired bicycles at the M. S. V. Cycle Mart. He worked as a newspaper boy for the Travancore news agency. He even sold combs, needles, and mirrors by the side of the road. He sold the "Shamana Prakashini" cure for indigestion. He earned commissions fetching clientele from the bus stand for local hotels. Finally, at the age of twenty-two, he got a job at Pillai's textile store. By then, he had already saved over three hundred rupees.

Finding employment at Pillai's store was a pivotal moment in Khader's life. He worked there for about five years. Those five years held a particular significance in his life story. It was during those years that he found some stability. Until then, he had been jumping from job to job, moving from place to place. But now he wanted to focus and master a trade, learn all its nuances. He was tired of running around, always out in the sun and rain. He now wanted somewhere cool and indoors to do his work, and those five years showed Khader that he wanted it for the rest of his life.

Fate sent him Mahadanapuram Gopala Iyer. Khader happened to hear that Gopala Iyer was planning to open a new textile store. On a Friday, when Pillai's store was closed, he met with Gopala Iyer under the pretext that he was in the area to collect payments from someone in Velangudi. The meeting with Iyer allowed Khader not only to confirm the rumors but also to size up the man.

On his way back through the fields to the bus stand, Khader could not help but chuckle to himself as he thought of the meeting. He was hatching a plan.

⋊

Gopala Iyer had a reputation for taking risks and doing things spontaneously. When he was young, he had enlisted in the military even though there was really no need for him to do so. At that time, his father was the richest man in the village. After a serious argument with his father, he left a suicide note and ran away from home. This was during World War II. He headed straight to the military and enlisted. It was not as if he had had a change of heart and decided that it was better to die fighting for the British Empire than to end his own life. In fact, it had never been his intention to commit suicide—not even when he wrote that note. He just wanted his mother and father to suffer as much as possible, believing that their son had taken his own life. But the irony was that his father was completely unperturbed by that letter. "I have looked at Gopala's horoscope. There is no chance for a suicide at the moment," he said, and thought no more about it. The villagers had their own story about what happened next. Apparently, Gopala Iyer wrote to his father from Chota Nagpur, asking for some money, and the father wrote back, "Since you have committed suicide, you won't be able to sign for the money." We don't know if there is any truth to this story.

When he was thirty years old, Gopala Iyer returned to the village early one morning, decked in military attire, a hat, and sunglasses. He had become quite stout. The sun had darkened his skin. Early baldness had encroached to the middle of his head. His lips had grown dark like they'd been roasted over a fire. And there was a whiff of aggression in his speech. Even five or six years after his return, no one in the village was ready to offer their daughter in marriage to him. By then, both his parents had passed away. This was how Gopala Iyer spoke of his father's death: "Well, when he was alive he said he wouldn't give me a penny. But now he has left everything to me."

Gopala Iyer couldn't quit some of the habits he had acquired in the military. His palate seemed to reject vegetarian food, and it also needed alcohol now and then. Men in the village gave him a wide berth because they were afraid of his sharp tongue. But the women were his ardent admirers. They laughed heartily at everything he said. He often plonked himself down at the entrance to his house and made fun of passersby. He once stood in front of the village priest's house and called out, "Hey, Narayana Sastrigal! Give me a sacred thread, if you've got an extra one, will you? I can't think of a more convenient way to scratch my back." He delighted in these scandalous things, even courting women from castes and communities below his. Once, when he encountered Aravalai from the Paraiyar community carrying a bundle of grass, he said to her, "Listen, Aravalai. I am going to give it just one more year. If none of these fellows is ready to marry his daughter to me by then, I shall marry your daughter. My mind is made up." When he said such things, women ran back into their houses, their hands clasped over their mouths.

Nevertheless, Aravalai never got the chance to have Gopala Iyer for her son-in-law. The country was ravaged by famine, and women were a bargain. If you could count on having enough food to eat, then you were among the most fortunate, and parents lined up to marry their daughters to you. Anandam Ammal did exactly that in marrying her daughter to Gopala Iyer. People said to Anandam Ammal, "Your daughter is only fifteen years old, and she is pretty as a parrot. Do you really plan to give her in marriage to that forty-year-old baldy?!" She simply replied, "Well, if she is destined to have a strong marriage, he will live long. Or else she will drape herself in a widow's veil, a silk one at that, and enjoy rice and warm milk for the rest of her life."

Gopala Iyer went to buy his wedding clothes at a shop run by a Sindhi family in Madurai. It was a big purchase, and so he had to spend four or five hours in that shop. As soon as he entered, the sight of Daulat Ram seated on a large cushioned sofa made a strong impression on him. A ceiling fan whirled overhead, and Daulat Ram sat under it, clutching a cigar between his teeth. The fine gold chain he wore around his neck dangled in front over his unbuttoned kurta. His eyes were bloodshot, and Gopala Iyer knew the reason: alcohol. But Daulat Ram was such a picture of composure that you would think he'd just come from having a dip in the holy Ganges and that was why his eyes were red. His words, his actions, everything about him was calculated and precise. His eyes were in constant motion, surveying everything in their vicinity. Even as his hand reached to receive a payment, his mind was already totaling the bill. When he was on the phone with somebody, his throat laughed, but his face scowled to issue some command, his eyes glared at the shop boy, and he even smiled at a customer and winked at a little girl. When a child started crying, he made a face at the shop boy, who then immediately ran out and came back with a packet of cookies for the kid. Gopala Iyer felt he could sit there all day watching that man in action. Suddenly there was a phone call from Bombay, and Daulat Ram began to speak in English. Gopala Iyer was totally entranced by the way he spoke. "The man's an absolute king!" he said to himself. He wanted to tell everybody back in the village about him. And he could not help but wonder how wonderful it would be if it were he sitting on that cushioned sofa.

On his way back home on the train, he read from *Dare to Act*, an English title he had picked up at the station. Captivated by the feeling that he was engaged in some serious intellectual pursuit, he also smoked cigarette after cigarette. Every sentence in that book expressed what was already in his mind. Yes, fortune indeed favors the brave! Persistence alone bears fruit! No doubt at all. He then initiated a conversation with the people sitting across from him, somehow steering the exchange toward what he was thinking, manipulating them into taking a contrary position, and then speaking against theirs. "We can't simply be envious of the white man because he prospers. Only those who dare to act will succeed. But we are too afraid to get in the water because we think it is cold!" he shouted.

By the time he got off at the Tirunelveli station, a firm resolve had formed in his mind. Even on the bus to Nagercoil, the same insistent thoughts roiled around in his sleep-addled mind.

. . . *All right, I don't deny that you are smart. Indeed, you are exceptionally smart,* he addressed the merchant Daulat Ram. *That lively face of yours! Your eyes and your hands and your lips, they are constantly busy, getting things done. That lucky face of yours is sure to charm both men and*

women and draw them to your store. I don't deny any of this. The moment
you wake up in the morning, Goddess Lakshmi is likely to be sitting by your
feet, pouring gold and silver and grains from her large measuring bowls.
I don't deny that either. That's how beautifully your stars are aligned. But
none of this means you are the only one destined to enjoy these fortunes.
There's always a place for anyone who is smart and skillful, who has a vision,
and who speaks well. Such people can thrive anywhere. Imagine such a
man. Now perhaps Goddess Lakshmi might shower him with a little less
gold and silver. But that still does not mean you are the smartest among
them all. That thought, that sense of "I am the best, there is no one like
me," that's not very becoming, you know? Not just for you, for anyone. That's
why I am telling you this. Look, I have decided to open my own store. But
don't pooh-pooh it. Don't say, "That's nothing! Such a small store." So what
if it is not a big business? I have some means. Let's assume I sell ten bushels
of paddy and use that as capital. Then, if the time is right and everything
works out, I might make a little profit. Then I will invest that profit again.
What? You think I can't do it? I have ten years of military experience. I
speak beautiful English. No, no, I am not saying your English isn't good.
You speak well, and your pronunciation is just like a white man's. Sure, go
ahead and believe that. But my English sounds exactly like a white man's!
You'll see what I plan to do. Listen, how about this? One of these days, for
Holi or Deepavali, you might take your wife and children on a holiday to
Kanyakumari, right? Nagercoil is just on the way. Why don't you stop and
ask for Gopala Iyer's shop and come and pay me a visit? What? No? Why
not? You think it is beneath you? So what? I may not be equal to you, but
you can at least be curious to see how far I have come. What do you say? Do
you accept? Hey, I am talking to you! Are you so proud . . .

"Sir! You are muttering in your sleep," the conductor said, shaking
him. He turned to the rest of the bus and announced: "Clock tower,
clock tower!"

Within a month of his marriage, Gopala Iyer sold four bushels of
the harvest from his Terur fields. The word around town was that he had

already taken possession of a shop in Nagercoil. He first needed to procure his inventory, so he was looking for somebody experienced in these matters. A few people spoke highly of Khader in this regard, but they all felt there was no chance Khader would quit his job at Pillai's shop.

Fate smiled on Gopala Iyer! It so happened that Khader himself came to meet Iyer—he was in the area to collect payment from someone in Velangudi. What luck! Gopala Iyer took the opportunity to get a sense of Khader's thoughts on the subject—would he leave Pillai's textile shop and come work for Iyer? But Khader only said, "The owner treats me like his own son. So I cannot suddenly just up and leave and damage the relationship. But not to worry. You say you want to open in January. There is time to figure this out."

Over the next few days, Khader gave Gopala Iyer's offer some serious thought. In a way, it was like jumping from a ship to a raft. Besides, Pillai's ship had a solid anchor. He wasn't sure if Gopala Iyer's raft could withstand even a little wind and a few strong waves. He consulted a few close friends, and they advised against it. They all gave good reasons for their advice, and Khader agreed with them. Like them, Khader too believed that if he left, he might come to regret his decision sooner rather than later. But despite all these considerations, he still decided to quit his job at Pillai's shop.

Words cannot describe the shock and disappointment Pillai felt when Khader informed him of his decision. Even so, Pillai did not betray his emotions in any way; nor did he give Khader a direct response. Instead, he simply said, "Come to my house Friday morning." He was afraid that if he continued the conversation right then at the shop, he might end up saying things that would only strengthen Khader's resolve. Moreover, Khader had no idea how Pillai truly felt about him. When they were in the store, he treated Khader just like he treated the other boys who worked there. And that was as it should be. But the time had come for Pillai to open his heart. He truly believed that once he expressed himself clearly, Khader would feel no need to insist on his decision.

On Friday, Pillai explained everything in detail to Khader.

"Khader, you know my story. I don't need to tell you. When my older son, Raja, told me categorically that he wanted nothing to do with the shop and went away to Madras, I considered closing down the business. But I could see that you were good at this work. You were already running around picking up merchandise, and you were skilled at selecting the stock. Once my younger son, Mani, finishes tenth grade, I am going to stop his education and start him out in the store. Until today, I had been thinking that, even if I am remiss in my supervision, you will look after him and run the business smartly. I have even written up a contract—once I stop overseeing things here, you will get a quarter of every rupee of profit we make for the first ten years. You know all the accounts up to date, how much profit we make, and what principal we reinvest. So you do the math. Mani will join you next year. I am tired of watching over things. So you please take him under your wing and keep our store's reputation going . . ."

Khader kept his head lowered and did not look up at Pillai.

"The very first time you came to the shop looking for a job, I told you to open a towel and fold it up again properly. You struggled with it. You were so worried I'd send you away, you had tears in your eyes. Please remember that. I am not trying to say such talents are determined by birth and only my sons can do it. You've learned so many things since. You have thought of this as your own store, and you have worked very hard. You spoke so much about Bombay and convinced me to send you there to buy stock. The business has certainly improved since; I am not denying that. But think about it. Anybody would agree it's not a good idea to leave a place you know so well. You don't know Gopala Iyer. He changes his mind in a flash. Please speak to a few people you are close to. Don't trust a clay horse to help you cross the river. Also, if you are upset about something, please speak to me frankly. We can work it out. Don't worry about anything . . . I am not the type who values money over everything else."

Khader looked away and didn't say a word.

"You came down with typhoid, and I sent the shop boys to look after you. I called the doctor every day, morning and night, to find out how you were doing. The man even teased me. 'Are you planning to adopt this boy?' he asked me. His fee as well as the medical expenses, I paid both out of my pocket. I never told you how much it cost, and I am not telling you even now . . . You also know that I am not like this with everyone. I did it because I care for you. All I can say is, it is not good for you to leave me feeling hurt, believing that you have deserted me after all these years of working together . . ."

Khader lowered his head again.

"Now, look! You don't need to feel bad about anything now. I am sure that man sweet-talked you into considering his offer, and you feel tempted. That's all there is to it. And you are not alone in thinking that elsewhere must be better than where you are right now. It's human nature to think that way. So don't worry if you have made me think less of you after all these years of honest work. I will consider this entire episode as a bad dream and forget about it. You know my nature. I am not the kind to keep something hidden in my mind and just act out. So go wash your face and get back to work as usual . . ."

Khader quickly walked away, opened the door, and left.

"Poor fellow," Pillai murmured to himself. "He is a good boy. Someone's tempted him and got him all confused. Why can't they just let a person be committed to where he is and make something of himself?"

At nine o'clock the next morning, Pillai called the store to speak to the accountant, asking him to send someone to fetch the bundles that had arrived at the lorry office and to have Khader price the new

Puliyankudi saris. But the accountant said, "Khader has not shown up for work yet." Pillai came over immediately. As soon as he got to the store, he sent someone over to Khader's room. The boy returned to tell him the room was locked. That same evening, Pillai learned that Khader had gone to Chennai with Gopala Iyer to buy stock for his new shop.

Initially, Gopala Iyer was very enthusiastic about his new venture. The cabinets and the counters in his shop were all of the latest fashion. A row of ceiling fans hung overhead. A telephone sat on his table. And he bought a swivel chair for himself. Whether or not there were any customers in the store, all the fans kept turning and all lights were always kept on. "We cannot keep turning each switch on and off all the time, can we? This is what we will do. We will keep all the switches on all the time. When we open the store in the morning, we will turn the main on, and we will turn it off when we close," said Gopala Iyer. He started ringing for the boy next door to run errands for him. I still remember what my friend Moolakkaraipatti Reddiyar—he had a restaurant close to Gopala Iyer's shop in those days—used to say about Iyer: "My business is going well, but it's never really crowded here. People eat coffee and snacks here and head straight over to Gopala Iyer's shop to look at clothes," he said, laughing as he wiped his armpits with a towel.

Khader got along very well with Gopala Iyer. One can't say he pushed back against even some of Gopala Iyer's most ill-conceived schemes, but he did assume full responsibility for running the shop. He traveled to buy new stock. He got checks signed by Gopala Iyer and punctually dispatched them to out-of-town merchants. He supervised the boys working in the shop, but there were also times he engaged with the customers directly, showing them the merchandise. He managed the accounts and went in person to the income-tax and sales-tax offices to declare the revenue.

Gopala Iyer came to place enormous trust in Khader. He was confident that he did not have to worry about the business at all and started spending a lot of time on the floor above Reddiyar's restaurant, playing cards with some serious gamblers. Every once in a while, he'd come to check on the store, and Khader would say to him, "You don't worry about a thing. I am in charge here." They made good profit that first year.

But in due course, it came to a point where Gopala Iyer had no idea what was going on with his shop. He had to speak to Khader to clarify even the most basic queries about his business. He could not answer any questions from customers; Khader had to deal with that too. If anyone asked him about pending payments, he needed Khader to decide if and when the checks should be sent. He realized this situation was pathetic, and it gave him a nagging sense of inferiority.

One day, a merchant from out of town came into the shop. When he found that Khader was not around, he said, "Oh, the owner is not here? No worries. I will come back later," and started walking away.

Gopala Iyer was irate. "Hey, you!" He clapped his hands. "Come back here."

The man turned around.

"Who do you think is the owner?"

"The man who is usually here. The fair-skinned one. He buys wholesale from me."

"Get over here!"

The man stepped into the shop.

"Why are you here?"

"I have brought samples to show."

"Show them to me."

The man spread out the samples on the counter.

"We will take two bolts per piece."

"Which ones?"

"The ones you just showed me."

"All of them?!"

"Yes, all of them."

"You will be able to sell that much?"

"Why do you need to know?"

"I was just curious."

"You don't need to be curious. Just write down the order. I will sign for it."

Luckily for him, half of that order sold out fast. But the other half just sat there. Gopala Iyer took great pains to unload it. He only showed merchandise from that order to all the customers. But it would not sell.

One day, when Khader had stepped out for lunch, one of the shop boys said to Gopala Iyer: "When you are not in the store, Khader won't show that stock to the customers. He won't let us show it either."

"Listen to me carefully. Whoever comes in, make sure you show my stock first. Doesn't matter what he does," he ordered.

From then on, Gopala Iyer never budged from his spot. "Just you wait and see. I will set that boy straight," he kept saying to himself. This time, he went in person to purchase the new inventory. At the Chennai warehouses, he learned that Khader had been pocketing a commission in cash for every purchase of stock he made. This piece of information came from a Pillai fellow from Tirunelveli, who had left a leading merchant and was now running his own little restaurant. The man also told Gopala Iyer that his former boss refused to accept Khader's arrangement, and so Khader never bought any stock from him. On that trip, Gopala Iyer procured a massive inventory. In fact, it was twice as much as Khader usually procured. His plan was to get the entire stock priced soon and to sell everything by Deepavali. So he hired a lorry to transport everything from Chennai, and he took a flight to Thiruvananthapuram, where he hired a taxi to take him all the way to his shop.

Gopala Iyer did excellent business during the Deepavali season that year. There was not enough space inside the shop to hold all the customers, and people had to wait outside on the steps. Two days before Deepavali, people started jostling and shoving and pushing to get into the shop. You would think they were getting the stuff for free! Gopala

Iyer stood in front of the counter, welcoming everyone. A steady stream of boys from the restaurant kept bringing coffee and tea and cool drinks and leaving with empty cups. Daulat Ram's face appeared in Gopala Iyer's mind. He imagined the man standing in front of the store, taking in the scene. *What are you so surprised about? Nothing much to see. Yes, I am running my business. But nothing you haven't seen. Yes, it is going all right. True, it is all by God's grace. Everything happens by His grace. Everything. Don't think this is all my doing. It's all His grace.*

Gopala Iyer continued to do the purchasing himself. When they took inventory that year, they found that they still had fifty thousand rupees' worth of stock. So Gopala Iyer tried to keep the new purchases in check. But he couldn't. "What's this, sir? Last time you bought stuff worth four or five thousand rupees. Now you want to spend only one or two thousand?" He couldn't bear the taunts from the wholesale merchants. So, just to save face, he again bought a huge stock. The thought of Khader, who had mentally detached himself from the running of the store and only made a show of being upset by things, enraged Gopala Iyer. He was convinced that Khader was, in truth, laughing at him. "Go ahead, laugh," he kept muttering to himself. "My horoscope says I will be rid of Saturn by August. There's no holding me back after that."

After Gopala Iyer ordered the stock, he paid back the credit in installments for the next few months. Because he was anxious to pay back the loans from the bank, and because he felt he could not afford to lose any customers, he started selling items at bargain prices. Despite all these efforts, one of his checks bounced. Within the next half an hour, the news spread through the entire warehouse district. One after another, the wholesale agents arrived at his shop. Suddenly, now these agents had a different attitude! A whole different tone of voice! These were the same men who had once fawned over him, who'd been so obsequious not long ago. "There's a step over there, be careful!" "Low entrance, please bend down!" "Let me carry your handbag, sir." All that was now gone. These very same men used to bring him sweets in banana-leaf parcels and say, "This is a new sweet. Try this, sir." Now they were saying, "Sir, honor and pride are the most important things for a man." The folks at the bank had no compassion for him—not only did they refuse to issue any further credit, but they took him to court for the outstanding debt, plus the interest. Gopala Iyer had to sell the fields he had earlier mortgaged. Khader managed to pawn some of Gopala Iyer's wife's jewelry and brought him some cash. Afraid of being besieged by his creditors, Gopala Iyer didn't leave his house anymore. The wholesale agents started gathering in front of his house every morning, effectively blocking him from going anywhere.

All his friends advised him to sell the store. He was eager to get it all over with as quickly as possible.

Khader told him about a Muslim businessman from Melapalayam who had made his fortune in Colombo. Apparently, he had approached Khader about the possibility of going into business together. If Gopala Iyer was willing to sell his business to this man, Khader could then join him. Gopala Iyer agreed.

They settled quickly on the details. Gopala Iyer would be offered a down payment of twenty-five thousand rupees, followed by seven hundred rupees per month for twenty-three months, not including interest. Gopala Iyer signed the deal, took his down payment, and moved back home to Mahadanapuram.

Within days, he learned that there was no Muslim businessman from Melapalayam, no fortune from Colombo. Khader had sole possession of the store; he had paid the entire down payment himself, in cash, from all the commission he had made over the years.

Khader had become a business owner. His dream had come true.

He felt that leaving Pillai's store and joining Gopala Iyer had been a very judicious move. Now, he was simply amazed at his own acumen and foresight.

10.

It was through his wife that Khader came to own the stationery shop that was right next to the tamarind tree. Just as he had dreamed when he was younger, he ended up marrying the only daughter of a rich man.

At a very young age, Janab Abdul Aziz had left Kalakkad for Singapore and returned when he was fifty, a few lakhs richer. He came back to Kalakkad to retire, dreaming of spending the rest of his life in pleasant inactivity and rest. However, as someone who had worked hard since childhood, it was not long before he realized that retirement was a punishment, not a reward. He learned that if he invested some of his money in vacant plots of land, he might garner excellent returns when they increased in value over the years. So he bought a small plot at the tamarind-tree junction from Neelakantan Potri, for eighty rupees a cent. Later, he decided to build a shop there so he could rent it out. Many people in Kalakkad began to express their interest in renting the store even before construction was complete, which showed him how in demand that location was. And it made him wonder. *Well, I am dying of boredom here,* he thought. *Why don't I do something myself?*

Once the construction was over, he furnished the store with the bare essentials, so sparsely that anyone looking in from the outside would assume the store was empty. And there he sat. The time passed agreeably. Why wouldn't it? It was, after all, the tamarind-tree junction. Newspapers landed at his doorstep every morning and evening. He had hired a few boys to boss around. There was a cinema theater right next door. The non-veg restaurant was just a few feet away. And there were his friends from the Muslim League to discuss politics.

But business never caught on. His political views were the reason why. The first thing anyone would see as they climbed the steps to the store was a huge portrait of Janab Jinnah Sahib, once the leader of the Muslim League and then the first governor-general of Pakistan. What other reason did the nationalists need to boycott the shop? He could always consider lowering the prices, but the trouble was that Janab Abdul Aziz was not a man of tact. Like an old man singing his first wife's praises to his second wife, he endlessly glorified Singapore and spoke unflatteringly of India to everyone. So it was no surprise that his business never took off.

That was the state of things when Khader and Janab Abdul Aziz became acquainted with each other. It started when Aziz visited Khader's store to buy clothes. He was very impressed with Khader's business acumen and how he conducted himself. In due course, it became a habit for him to head over to Khader's shop whenever he was not busy. On one occasion, Khader asked to borrow some money to clear a waybill from the bank, since he was short of cash. Aziz helped him because he trusted him as a fellow Muslim. On another occasion, when Khader sent for money again and promised to return it in two months, Aziz sent the amount without expressing his misgivings. Khader immediately sent him a signed promissory note attesting to one percent interest. Aziz was very pleased with that. Exactly sixty days later, he got the initial amount plus interest. There were a few more transactions like this, and soon, lending and borrowing became a formal business transaction between them. When he received the principal and the interest on the due date, Aziz would roar with laughter and say, before locking away the money in the safe, "My, my! Never even a day late, huh? Let me make a note of it!"

On this return home to Kalakkad every week, Aziz could not stop talking about Khader to his wife. His wife perfectly understood the intentions behind this—Aziz wanted Khader for a son-in-law—but yet she wondered if Khader was truly as handsome as her husband made him out to be.

One evening at dusk, Khader came to Aziz's store in a hurry.

"Uncle, I have come to discuss a business idea with you," he said.

Representatives from the Bombay Quality Tobacco Company had arrived in town that day. The main objective for their visit was to appoint a local agent for their product. A lot of interested people were already beginning to swarm around them. Khader urged Aziz to try and secure the agency.

"Good God! I am not up to it at all," Aziz said immediately.

"Uncle, please don't drag your feet on this. Such lucky breaks don't come around often. You just need to put in two years of hard work. Then the money will start pouring in."

"I cannot deal with all the hassles, not at my age. I'll have to do all the advertising. I'll have to go store to store, begging for business. I'll have to hire sub-agents. I'll have to rent a warehouse. Then these guys will pay visits to check the stock, and I'll have to fawn over them endlessly. No way. Too much hassle."

"Uncle, I tell you, this is a good product. If we find the right market for it, it will sell itself. Over in Malabar, they don't smoke anything but Camels . . ."

"I get it. But these fellows who smoke, they are not of steady mind. In an instant, they will drop the Camels and jump over to Horses. And there we are, braving the desert, trusting our Camels . . ."

"Please be serious, Uncle. All you need to do is say yes. You won't even have to get up from this chair. I will get this done. You've got some extra cash. If you put a little of it into this venture, you'll be supporting ten of our own people. As it is, 'our' place here is not secure. If we leave all new ventures to others, they will make sure we are forever selling nothing but soaps and combs and tin boxes. They already look down on us . . ."

"You feel so strongly about this, why don't you take it up yourself?"

"Uncle, why tease me when you know my situation? If I had that kind of money, I wouldn't be asking you to do it."

"Are you really that short of money? Come on, don't give me that."

"Look at your loan books again if you don't believe me. Come on, Uncle. If I take ten or twenty thousand rupees out of the current flow, I will never be able to put it back. You know that, Uncle . . ."

"All right. Do this, then. Go ahead and take the deal. I will give you the money."

"Are you joking with me?"

"I am not joking at all! Bring me a contract specifying the installments that will work for you, and I will give you the money. Put down an interest rate you can handle—we don't need to discuss it."

"What are you talking about?"

"Why do you keep asking me what I am talking about? You said you'd take the deal if you had the money. I've told you I will give you the money. Why are you still pestering me about this?"

"We need a place to . . ."

"Right here, this store."

"What about you?"

"I will move over to a corner! Some business this is. It's not like I will be losing anything. Everything I have will fit into two trunks. A single coolie could haul it all away."

Out on the street, Khader felt like he was walking on air. He was suddenly reminded of his father. *This must be the result of his endless prayers,* he thought. As his father's face swam across his mind, his eyes welled up with tears.

Khader closed the deal successfully. The first smart thing he did was invite the company representatives to the Cosmopolitan Hotel in Kanyakumari. This way, he was able to cut them off from the useless crowd that was always hovering around them, even though it had nothing to offer. Khader made himself available to serve those representatives

116

to their satisfaction. He attended to their every need skillfully and with discretion, leaving nothing to chance. The impression they got was that, even though he liked to have fun, he was someone who would get things done. They also believed that he would bring his youthful energy to the job.

However, after everything was talked over and talked through, there was a shock in store for Khader. The director would only accept the offer if it were Khader's own money, complete with bank statements—not borrowed money. It was an unforeseen death blow.

"My uncle is providing the capital. Won't that do?" he asked.

"Your own uncle?"

"My mother's second cousin. He is just like a father to me. I consult him on everything."

The others present there tried to reason with the director, but to no avail.

Asking for twenty-four hours to sort things out, Khader left.

Next day, however, he told Aziz, "It's almost finalized. The contract needs to be drawn. It looks like I'll have to sign a thousand documents. So much paperwork . . ."

"Khader, I wanted to talk to you about something else," began Aziz.

"What is it?"

"Nothing serious. You see, ever since we got acquainted, I have been talking about you to my wife all the time. It seems I was mentioning your name a lot one day. My wife suddenly said to me, 'You talk about him so much! What's your plan? Are you thinking of making him your son-in-law?' I said to her, 'Well, yes . . . perhaps.' Turns out she took my word for it. Long story short, she wants the wedding to happen within the year . . ."

"Uncle! What?! Are you serious? This sounds crazy . . ."

"Well, think of me as a little crazy!"

"Uncle, I don't know what to say. These days, our boys are getting BA and MA degrees. If you are willing to give a dowry of even ten or twenty thousand rupees, you will find an excellent man for your daughter."

"Khader, don't forget, I made my money in business, just like you. If you underestimate yourself, you are doing the same of me."

Khader grew silent.

"What happened? Are you worried that you have not seen the girl? Do you want to see her?" asked Aziz.

"Uncle, what are you saying? That's not our custom."

"Just brush that all aside. I don't want to hear about the customs of our wretched people. Do you think that my daughter is a woman of the veil? Do you know of anyone in our community who has taken his wife and daughter on a ship? I took them with me thirty years ago. My entire village was against it. 'To hell with you, you fools,' I said to them before I got on the boat. 'Over there, your sons and sons-in-law are running after Chinese women!' She grew up in Singapore. If you come over one day, she will serve you tea and also size you up in one glance. That's the kind of girl she is."

Khader went to Kalakkad that evening. He found the girl utterly ugly. Had she taken after her father, she could have been quite beautiful. But even if she had taken after her mother, there was no reason for her to be so horrid. Khader thought of *his* mother. He also thought of the woman who had entranced him at the Krishnan temple festival, whose mother had served her naked to him after taking fifty rupees from him. He also thought of the beautiful faces and bodies of all the women he had been with since then. A wave of despair rose to choke him. Stunned and distracted, he sat on a stool at the back of his store. The phone call came from Kanyakumari on behalf of the director. "I will give you all the details tomorrow morning. Expect no further delay," he promised them.

He ran over to Aziz's store. He told him the entire matter. "I almost had it in my hands. But it has slipped away."

Aziz sat silently for a few minutes. Then he said, "Khader, there is nothing to worry about. You will have the passbook in your hands by ten tomorrow morning."

"What?!"

"It will be in your name! From now on, we are one, aren't we? So this turned out well."

Khader was at a loss for words. He sat still.

"Khader, don't you like my daughter?" asked Aziz, smiling.

Khader did not respond; he couldn't. Without a word, he left and walked slowly back to the tamarind-tree junction.

11.

Khader's new store did the best business in the tamarind-tree junction. He seemed to have taken over that store from his now father-in-law, Aziz, at the most opportune moment. He started a wholesale and retail stationery store, and it really thrived. Despite his goodwill gestures in the sale of the textile store he'd owned earlier, he still made a great deal of money from it and invested all of it in this new store. Khader was not keen on a huge profit. He preferred to keep the goods moving at a moderate margin of profit. He wanted the store to be busy all the time. He was happy as long as he made two or three thousand rupees at the end of the day. How much of that amounted to a profit was of little concern to him.

Khader, his wife, and Aziz all settled down in a bungalow in Kottar. Even in the very first weeks of their marriage, Khader developed an intense aversion to his wife. Every part of her body was repellent to him. In his heart, he began to hope that she would just die. He yearned to be free of this shackle, so he could actually find someone to his liking and start a new and happy married life while he was still young. He knew that these were but futile dreams. Arguments and fights and abuses became their everyday affair. Aziz moved back to Kalakkad, unable to bear the sight of Khader horribly beating his pregnant daughter. He had lost his first wife some time back, and, unable to bear the loneliness, he married again. One look at his new bride sent Khader into a jealous rage. He hit his wife, screaming in disbelief that the old man had found such a beautiful wife. "Go! Go bring her here!" he screamed. His wife was by then accustomed to his drunken tirades. She had long since reached the point where even stabbing herself in the eye wouldn't cause her to shed a tear.

The failures of his marital life proved to be conducive to Khader's business. In an attempt to forget his domestic troubles, he started spending all his time at the store. He was like a man possessed, working with such tirelessness and frenzy that it looked like he was avenging himself. He started dreading the very prospect of free time and came up with constant work to stave off that possibility. Thanks to his drinking, he slept peacefully at night. Even though he was an unlucky fellow by his own estimate, he found some satisfaction in the fact that others considered him to be fortunate. He complained to his friends that the other merchants in the bazaar were jealous of him, but behind his guileless and anxious expression, he was secretly glad of it. He strove to achieve new successes that would stoke their flame of jealousy even more. He learned that some of his rivals had resorted to bad-mouthing him. "Wasn't this Gopala Iyer's investment originally?" they said, raking up his checkered past. Gopala Iyer had passed away by now, and Khader began to gift his family fifty rupees a month. On the first day of every month, without fail, he sent a boy to Mahadanapuram with the money. The opinion in the Brahmin quarter was that even if Gopala Iyer were still alive, there was no assurance his family would get that much money for their expenses every month. Even Gopala Iyer's wife started singing Khader's praises. Considering that no one who stole another's business had ever done something so virtuous, Khader was, in a way, worthy of that praise.

Truth be told, the cigarette agency he obtained with his father-in-law's help was the reason Khader had reached new heights. Gone were the days when, at temple festivals and fairs, free cigarettes had to be thrown from trucks at crowds to entice them and a long lecture delivered over a loudspeaker about the uniqueness of Camel-brand cigarettes. Now people were hooked, and all betel merchants from Parvatipuram to Anappalam had to jostle at Khader's store to purchase their stock. Seeing so many people throng to his store made Khader arrogant. The poise that had characterized his speech and demeanor over the years now wavered. He started being dismissive of people who traveled three miles by bicycle just to come to his shop, offering lame excuses for not being able to attend to them right away and asking them to come back later. "If you want to get some gold, you need to be serious about it. You need to be patient." This became a mantra he repeated a hundred times a day.

In time, once the Betel Merchants' Association was formed, the shopkeepers whom Khader turned away for ridiculous reasons started bringing Dhamu the shopkeeper with them for support. Deep down, Khader was scared of Dhamu. He knew Dhamu was a tough man, so he wanted to be on his good side.

$$\mathfrak{X}$$

Years later, I painstakingly gathered accounts of the history of enmity between Dhamu and Khader. In those days, I was overcome with disappointment that India had gained independence without giving me an opportunity to play any part in it. Perhaps as a distraction from that, I joined my friends in being curious about everything concerning Dhamu, our local shopkeeper and freedom fighter. Uninvited, I inserted myself in the various groups that discussed the scandal in the many corners of the bazaar and listened attentively. I didn't know enough then to be bothered by the looks of disdain the older folks gave me—all I wanted was to find out information my friends didn't know, so that I could be the first to tell them. How I studied the expressions of the older men when they discussed these matters! I did my best to let those expressions animate my face too. I appropriated their opinions and turns of phrase and uttered them as my own. For some reason, it was very important to me to be seen as a responsible person, as someone who was deeply concerned about declining times.

When I sat in my back garden and retold all that I had learned to my sisters, I exaggerated events without even being conscious of it. If I was describing episodes of daring action, I embellished them to keep them exciting. I found great satisfaction in narrating things the way I wished them to have occurred or had imagined them to have happened. Even now, as I tell you about the life and death of the tamarind tree, I cannot claim to have completely freed myself from this tendency. Trying to fit our imagination to the realities of the world is an impossible task. All we can do is find some satisfaction in forcing the world to submit to our imagination instead. It seems that we are forever destined to carve our feet to fit our shoes.

But so what? After all, this wretchedness goes by the name of art these days, and so all is immediately forgiven. Besides, we all have learned to pretend to believe in the things we read at least while we are reading them, so that we may derive pleasure from them and dismiss everything else as lies. So no real harm done here.

Dhamu was from a family of five brothers, originally from Kuzhithurai. The children had been orphaned when their mother ran off with the healer who had been treating her stomachaches. Not only had their mother left her family, but she had gone off with a man from a lower caste, which was even more disgraceful. Soon after, the oldest, Chellappan, stopped a lorry on its way from an estate and hoisted his four brothers onto the back, and all of them had ended up in Nagercoil. I only knew three of the brothers. Chellappan only cared about the store; nothing else interested him. Dhamu was a patriot from the August Movement. He had been clubbed by the police at the clock-tower junction for refusing to take off his turban. That was when everyone came to know who he was. In those days, people considered it a veritable service to the nation to buy fruits from Dhamu's shop. Students would pass a hundred stores to get to his.

But there was another reason for my personal fascination with these brothers: Chellappan and Dhamu shared a wife. To me, this was an exotic and titillating arrangement. Others praised it as a smart way for the brothers to keep their income in one piece. I was curious to know if the arrangement caused any friction in their family and work life, but I found out that was not the case. Chellappan worked during the day; Dhamu took the night shift—this was how they divided their life. Dhamu's shop had no shutters. On the day Gandhiji was assassinated, they hung a black shawl to cover the entrance; this was the first time that shop had ever been closed since it started. The only time Chellappan and Dhamu were seen together was when they all went to Pazhani for a head-tonsuring ceremony for one of the kids.

Sukumaran was my source of information about Dhamu's and Chellappan's lives; he was the youngest of Dhamu's brothers and my classmate in school. Since I was obsessed with their family lives and wanted to learn more, I was close with Sukumaran. I still vividly remember going to their house one day on the pretext of borrowing a copy of Savarkar's *Volcano*. Sukumaran's sister-in-law—Dhamu and Chellappan's wife—was incredibly voluptuous. She had an insane figure. Very healthy and thriving. Sukumaran said to me, "Both my brothers vie with each other to feed her by hand. She knows how to enjoy her food." Apparently, both brothers were absolutely adamant that nobody else should watch her eating. Sukumaran also told me that his sister-in-law had become addicted to alcohol, a habit she'd picked up while recuperating after giving birth: "When Dhamu asked her if she knew Gandhiji had asked people not to consume alcohol, she said, 'That's only for men.'" Some of her children looked like Chellappan, and some looked like Dhamu. There were also children who looked like her, and so their father was a mystery. In school, I felt sorry for them. Imagine not knowing for sure who your father was! But now, with the wisdom of years, I know that the idea of chastity is not as entrenched as we imagine. A mother is the only irrefutable foundation of human birth. What else is a father but the sign of our trust in our mother's testimony?

The success of Dhamu's business was very well known. There was always a crowd in front of his shop. If the shop next door sold eight bananas for a panam, Dhamu sold six for the same price. No haggling was entertained. If anyone pointed out the price at the shop next door, both brothers retorted, "Well, go buy them over there then!" Neither of them cared how many customers there were, or how much of a hurry people were in. They had the same style of working; they took their own sweet time to take things off the shelves. But still, their shop was where the crowds went. The brothers attributed this good luck to their wife, even though neither of them would ever say it out loud.

Dhamu's shop was one of the tamarind-tree junction's key attractions. Indeed, the only other store in the region that did better business than Dhamu's was Khader's store. As Khader grew more and more unhappy with his marriage and more focused at work, shopkeepers from the Betel Merchants' Association began bringing Dhamu along so that Khader would listen to their requests. On one such occasion, Dhamu came to vouch for a shopkeeper by the name of Arumugam. Khader was in a strange frame of mind that day, and he decided he wouldn't be cowed down. So he said, "This man might be your brother-in-law, but that doesn't mean I have to show him special respect. I can't go bring you the stuff myself. You'll have to wait for my man to show up."

Enraged, Dhamu raised his hand to hit Khader. The bookkeeper jumped between them, which was the only reason why Khader escaped being beaten that day. He hadn't really put much thought into those words. He'd been angry and irritated about something else, and his words came out the way they had. But he had mentioned the secret affair between Dhamu and Arumugam's widowed sister, and so Dhamu was beside himself with anger. When things got really ugly, Khader changed his tactic. He said that Arumugam had a small outstanding balance on earlier purchases. "Let him clear that. Then I will give him the cigarettes," said Khader.

"So only those without any outstanding payments can purchase cigarettes from you?" Dhamu asked, to which Khader replied, "That's my decision." Dhamu glared at him and walked out of the shop. As soon as the news of this incident reached Aziz in Kalakkad, he dropped everything and headed to Khader's store. He stood outside the store—Khader was away at the time—and railed and ranted against certain beggars whom he did not wish to name. He even made indirect and disparaging remarks about Dhamu's caste before taking the evening bus back to Kalakkad. He had been so caught up in his anger that it had not even occurred to him to visit his daughter.

That was the start of the enmity between Dhamu and Khader, and it only grew worse over the years. They clashed on several occasions, provoked each other, insulted each other. Once upon a time, I meticulously collected details of these instances. I no longer remember many of them now, but one instance is fresh in my memory.

When prohibition came into effect, it became nearly impossible to buy high-quality liquor in our town, so many had to travel weekly to Kollam. When he didn't have the time to make the trip himself, Khader sent coolie Ayyappan on this errand. Once, Dhamu caught Ayyappan red-handed right in front of Khader's store and reported him to the police, bottles of liquor and all. Khader started telling people that Dhamu bought alcohol from him regularly for his wife, and that this attempt to incriminate him was because Khader had failed to procure bottles for him a couple of times. Khader described it with an air of factuality, as if Dhamu had begged him for alcohol and told him that his wife would only open the door for him at night if he held up a bottle at her window. "It's my fault," Khader said to Dhamu's friends. "How many nights can our big brother spend on the porch?"

As for Dhamu, he grew agitated whenever anyone brought up Khader's name. "I swear, I will not die until I see him back again on the porch with a pan full of tobacco, rolling beedis!" he bellowed, thumping his chest. "His father used to sweep the courtyard at the mosque. But the son now travels in the comfort of a car. No wonder he is so full of himself."

How long can such festering hostilities keep smoldering and expressing themselves in small conflicts and confrontations?

One day, everything exploded.

A week or so before the parliamentary budget session was about to begin, there was a sudden undersupply of cigarettes in the market. Prices began to skyrocket. Shopkeepers started gathering at the tamarind-tree junction and in front of Khader's store before he opened in the mornings, hoping to buy cigarette stocks for their shops. But Khader dropped the supply. He saw this as the perfect chance to collect on outstanding accounts. "I am going to supply only to those who have fully settled their accounts," he said. Everybody owed a hundred or two hundred rupees. Where would they find that much cash so quickly?

One day, when hundreds of shopkeepers were waiting outside Khader's store, Dhamu ran down the stairs from his shop. "I will get you the stuff. Follow me," he said to them, and rushed up the stairs into Khader's shop. All the merchants climbed up after him, their feet stomping loudly against the rungs of the wooden ladder. Khader called the police on Dhamu. A few bigwigs intervened and kept Dhamu from retaliating. By the time the police arrived, the crowd had dispersed. The inspector was a friend of Khader's. After driving away the remaining loafers and the coolies still lingering, he whispered to Khader, "If you want to be smart about this, move your stock elsewhere. Don't be a fool."

The stock rooms upstairs were emptied that very night. When betel merchants arrived the next morning, Khader acted very polite and agreeable. He threw the key on the table in front of them and said, "Take whatever amount you want." He made sure he sent two boxes to Dhamu. Then he tried his best to incite the merchants against Dhamu.

"Dhamu is acting up because he wants it all for himself. You think he cares about you? If you asked him, 'Don't you think you should give at least half the stock to others?' what would Dhamu say? 'Give it all to me.'"

All this backbiting was in vain, though. Khader could not shake the faith the betel merchants held in Dhamu.

When coolie Ayyappan was in jail, Dhamu hired a lawyer for him through a friend and secretly backed his case. He decided that it would be good to have Ayyappan on his side, since the man had been Khader's long-standing worker and enjoyed his confidence. He planned to secure Ayyappan's loyalty once he was out of jail so that he could learn Khader's secrets. Ayyappan was already upset that Khader had not bailed him out, so he was planning to join Dhamu as soon as he was released. Then, when he learned that Dhamu had spent money on his defense, he felt even more aligned with him. Since the prosecution had no real evidence, Ayyappan was soon cleared of all charges.

As soon as he was freed, coolie Ayyappan headed straight to Dhamu's store to pick up a cigarette. Then he walked over to Khader's store and climbed up the stairs. He stood in front of Khader, cigarette dangling from his lips, and said, "She wants a tin of talcum powder."

Khader looked up and was stunned to see Ayyappan's whole new demeanor.

"Who wants?" asked Khader.

"Rani."

"Rani who?"

"Rani from East Street. The same Rani I brought to the Puliyankurichi Tourist Bungalow the other day."

Khader's face turned crimson. Without a word, he lowered his eyes and pretended to go over the accounts.

The shop boys milled around the counter, clueless as to what was going on.

"In fact, Parameswari, Chellammai, Krishnammai, Pankajam, everyone wants a tin of talcum powder each. 'Your boss drooled all over my face and then he just left! Go get some talcum powder, so I can cover it up.' That's what they are all saying," said Ayyappan.

Khader looked at Ayyappan with cold fury.

"Remember Mary from Mangala Street? Sly one, she is! I warned you not to get mixed up with her. Well, she wants two tins."

By now, the boys were quietly stepping back.

Khader got up without a word and left, defeated.

From that day on, Ayyappan spent all his time in front of Dhamu's shop. Whenever his friends gathered around, Dhamu said to him, "Ayyappan, what were you asking Khader the other day? Oil or comb or something? Come on, tell us!" Ayyappan would launch into the story about Khader's mistresses and the talcum powder right away. Every time he told that story, Dhamu laughed long and hard like it was the first time he was hearing it. When Ayyappan was done with the story, Dhamu slapped him genially on the back and said, "*Chee!* That's too much. You have become too cheeky!" Like a dog enjoying a pat from its master, Ayyappan would cheerfully receive Dhamu's slaps on his back. Once his friends left, Dhamu would toss a half-rupee coin toward him. "Go have some coffee." Ayyappan would take it and walk away.

When Khader brought down the cigarette supply, the Betel Merchants' Association convened an emergency meeting of its action committee. Dhamu gave a fiery speech at this meeting. Some members were of the opinion that the association should send a letter of warning to Khader, but Dhamu denounced this as a cowardly gesture and an insult to the association's standing. He also could not agree with the other suggestion that the association should form a committee to negotiate with Khader. He argued that the association should inform the cigarette company's Bombay headquarters of what had happened and get them to send one of their representatives to town. This way, they could learn about Khader's outrageous behavior and the cigarette agency could be taken off his hands.

Dhamu laid out his arguments in great detail. "We didn't cave to the mighty British Empire. Wouldn't it be a disgrace to surrender to a small foe like Khader?!" he asked, and the members applauded in agreement. Dhamu emphasized that he had no intention of securing the cigarette agency for himself and that, in fact, he was willing to stake his body, wealth, and soul—all three—in making sure that another member of the association took over the agency. The president of the association, Rajapandiya Nadar, stood up to clarify on behalf of all the members that nobody doubted Dhamu's integrity, so he should not hurt the association by imputing bad intentions to them. Dhamu expressed his apologies. Being excitable was one of his weaknesses, he said meekly, and asked for their forgiveness.

A telegram was sent to the Bombay headquarters, in the name of around three hundred members of the association. They also received a return telegram, stating that the company would send down a special representative within twenty-four hours.

Khader went to receive that representative at the Thiruvananthapuram airport. Dhamu, his minions, and Isakki, a reporter from the *Travancore Nesan*, all came by another car. Dhamu presented the representative with a garland of roses and welcomed him on behalf of the association.

The inquiry was conducted on the upper floor of Khader's store. One by one, the betel merchants entered the inquiry room and gave their statements. The representative made a detailed record of everyone's grievances. Dhamu testified that the stocks that Khader had entered as "sold" were in fact not sold, that they were being held in secret warehouses, and that he would be able to locate them if he was given two days' time.

The inquiry came to an end.

Khader was happy that he was not subjected to any further questions. He and his accountant had been up all night fixing the books, and Khader was delighted their efforts had not been wasted. When the representative disagreed with his strategy to misuse the agency in order to collect his outstanding dues, Khader accepted his guilt without reservation. He promised not to make any such mistakes in the future. On the whole, it seemed that the entire matter would simply be put to bed with nothing more than an official letter of warning from the company.

But around six o'clock that evening, the representative, who sat at the entrance to Khader's store, smoking a cheroot and looking out at the tamarind-tree junction, suddenly sat up and asked: "Khader, how do you feel about a trip to Kanyakumari?"

"Sure, with pleasure. Let me call for the car," Khader said, picking up the phone.

"Not in your car," the representative said. "The situation is still quite bad, and we shouldn't give any reason for idle gossip." He walked down the stairs and clapped his hands.

A taxi pulled up.

As Khader and the company representative got into the back seat, coolie Ayyappan walked over from Dhamu's shop and climbed in next to the driver.

"Hey, you! Get out!" said Khader.

"But, boss, he is the helper," said the driver.

"What do we care? Let him come," the representative urged.

The taxi passed the Kottaram fruit farm and then pulled over in front of an old building.

"Why are you stopping here?" asked Khader, but the driver did not respond.

"Be quiet and follow me," the representative said, and got out of the car. He climbed up the stairs, stood in front of the locked door, and turned to Khader. "Open the door."

Khader hesitated.

"At the moment, this is still between us. But if you refuse, I have the company's orders to call the police. Make a smart decision," the representative said.

Khader opened the door.

Only three days later, Khader heard from the company that his permit had been revoked. The Betel Merchants' Association made sure it became front-page news in the *Travancore Nesan*. For the next three days, Khader got blind drunk and lay tossing on a bed at the Cosmopolitan Hotel in Kanyakumari.

When he returned to his store four days later, a sign in front of Dhamu's store read "Camel Brand Cigarettes—Wholesale."

Given this history of animosity, Khader could not be entirely faulted for suspecting that Dhamu was the one who smashed his store sign. Of course he had to go to the police. Although the police didn't take him very seriously when he shared his suspicions with them, Dhamu's friends believed—though they never expressed it in public—that the police saw this as a good opportunity to get their own revenge on Dhamu, whom they had hated for years. Even if you ignored the fact that Dhamu had insulted and antagonized the police in the days of the freedom struggle, everyone in the bazaar also knew that no police sepoy or head constable could ever get a free piece of fruit or a beedi in Dhamu's shop.

When the municipality's formal complaint arrived at the police station, the inspector went in person to meet with the chairman, M. C. Joseph. The chairman shared with him his suspicions about the involvement of the municipal manual scavengers in the theft of the tamarind pods.

And so, the police concocted two cases. They said that the manual scavengers were the ones who threw stones at the tamarind tree, but that Dhamu had made use of that situation to smash Khader's store sign, hoping the blame would fall on the manual scavengers. They drafted two conveniently related charges. The police were also quite confident that coolie Ayyappan was the man Dhamu had employed to smash Khader's sign.

The news of Dhamu's arrest made headlines in the *Travancore Nesan*. The town was abuzz with excitement. Politically minded young men, as well as old freedom fighters who'd had to step aside to make way for new political trends, congregated by the tamarind-tree junction, in front of Lala Sweet Shop, by the clock tower, in the Vadaseri market, and in Kambolam in Kottar to discuss the news. They speculated about the many terrible and terrifying consequences that were soon to follow. This was what the local bigwigs opined: since Dhamu had a political background and carried extraordinary clout among betel merchants as the secretary of their association, and since he belonged to a community that was a minority in the region and had the reputation for being organized and unified, there would be serious repercussions. News spread that the next day there would a general strike supported by the Betel Merchants' Association, that all stores would remain closed, *and* that there would also be a protest gathering on the municipal grounds. It was also rumored that an emergency meeting of the Betel Merchants' Association was scheduled for midnight and that men had already been sent in a taxi to fetch the local MLA, who had gone to Thiruvananthapuram to attend the legislative assembly in session. It was rumored that the glass showcases in Khader's store had been smashed within an hour of Dhamu's arrest, but nobody could confirm it. It turned out to be just a rumor. But that did not stop many from ridiculing Khader for keeping his head down for a few days and not going to his store. From the way people talked, it seemed that they were delighted with the tense situation. Dhamu was released on bail on the third day, and some five hundred merchants gathered outside the courthouse to garland him. This time around, the *Travancore Nesan* printed Dhamu's photo as well.

The day after Dhamu came out on bail, the police arrested Comrade Madasami, a manual scavenger who had worked closely with lawyer Janardhanan in organizing the scavengers' union. They also arrested Madasami's wife, Madathi, who had assisted her husband in enlisting women scavengers to the union. Since Madathi was pregnant and was ready to give birth when she was arrested, she was immediately taken by ambulance to the government maternity hospital. A week later, she gave birth to a healthy baby, in the presence of a policewoman by her bedside.

A warrant was issued for coolie Ayyappan's arrest, but they couldn't catch him. He was on the run.

12.

Thanks to the efforts of the young lawyer and union activist Janardhanan, Madasami was released on bail. The same evening, a rally to condemn police brutality was held in front of the municipal building. No special efforts were made to raise bail for Madathi. Madasami agreed with his lawyer's counsel that it would be stupid to jeopardize the postnatal care the government was providing her. The *Travancore Nesan* printed that lawyer Janardhanan had issued a warning at this public rally: all manual scavengers would go on an indefinite strike until the case filed against Madasami and his wife was withdrawn. The newspaper also carried an editorial insisting that the workers must be given an immediate pay raise. Everyone could tell the editorial had been written by Isakki. Who else could fit in the phrase "revolutionary fire" so many times in just two paragraphs! He must have kept the fire truck at the ready while writing that editorial.

The manual scavengers' union had already sent a petition to the municipality demanding a pay increase. The *Travancore Nesan* also reported that according to the explanation provided by Janardhanan at the rally—which was presided over by Madasami—the arrests had occurred because the municipality feared the workers would go on strike to press their pay-raise demands. So, in an effort to thwart any such attempts, false allegations had been foisted on the main movers in the union, and they had been spirited away. Whether this was true or not, the accusation was definitely believable. There was no telling what tricks the cowardly municipality would resort to when it felt threatened. It could end up doing the most terrible things out of fear.

Coolie Ayyappan seemed to have vanished without a trace. The police hunted for him everywhere, but to no avail. Five or six weeks had passed, marked by events of great turbulence and profound significance: Khader's store sign was smashed, Dhamu was arrested and then released on bail, Comrade Madathi gave birth to a baby in government custody, young lawyer Janardhanan raised a war cry at a meeting presided over by Madasami, and a veritable flow of lava had issued forth from the editorial pages of the *Travancore Nesan*. But the entire police force was still struggling to catch one lone scoundrel—it had become a popular subject of mockery.

Many said that coolie Ayyappan had fled past Kadukkarai village and entered Tirunelveli district through a secret mountain pass. They believed the Travancore police would find it difficult to apprehend him until they secured the cooperation of the Tirunelveli police. Others acted like they had access to secret intelligence and surmised that he had boarded a ship to Sri Lanka. Dhamu, they claimed, had secured him secret passage. It could be true—anything was possible when it came to Dhamu. He had the intelligence and the courage to achieve whatever he set his sights on. Some even said that the *Travancore Nesan* printed a picture of coolie Ayyappan, along with a promised reward for information on his whereabouts, but I don't recall seeing it.

After ten years, Dhamu's name was once again on everyone's lips, just as it had been in the days of the August Movement. Was there any-one who did not marvel at his courage back then? What sort of man would refuse to take off his turban when asked to do so by a police superintendent (D. S. P. Achyutan Nair, if I remember correctly)! After all, the man hadn't asked one to cut his own throat! The crowd that had gathered at the clock-tower junction witnessed the whole scene. At ten in the morning, in broad light, four constables shoved Dhamu to the ground, surrounded him, and kicked him as hard as they could with their boots, like he was some plaything. It is the absolute truth that he refused to take off his turban right up to the end. No exaggeration. It is a different matter that his turban *fell* off and rolled to the side when he writhed in pain. Some people said they saw him crawl on the cement road toward the turban, coughing up blood but still determined to wear it. Now that is an exaggeration. I have heard from witnesses that he kept shouting "Bharat Mata Ki Jai!"—"Long live Mother India!"—until he lost consciousness, but he never stopped clutching the turban.

After that incident, whenever anyone referred to "the August hero," it was clear they meant Dhamu. Back in those days, there was no greater role model for the young people of our town. His turban never left his head after that. When he went to an important gathering or to speak at public meetings, the turban was on his head. A few imaginative boys in my school said that the only time Dhamu removed his turban and tied it around his waist was when he stood in front of a picture of Gandhiji. That struck me then—as it does now—as something they had conjured up; they had an active imagination in many such matters.

However, when independence finally happened, Dhamu felt utterly lost and despondent. He felt that his fame was fading away rapidly. The only thing more short-lived than people's passion was their memory. At a time when people might ask, at any moment, who M. K. Gandhi was, Dhamu shouldn't be surprised that they would forget his name. But he still took it personally. What is fame, after all? Isn't it simply the pleasure of being recognized by people we don't know? Only those who have experienced it would know how precious it is. It is an extraordinary pleasure, no doubt about it. There is nothing small about the pleasure you get when you walk down the road and hear whispers behind you; you see people pointing you out to others, telling them who you are, but you walk on, pretending not to have noticed. Seeing your photo printed in the newspaper with opinions gives you immense joy. Anyone can pretend that they have renounced such attachments. But pleasure is pleasure. You do feel thrilled when people garland you. When they applaud you. Dhamu had grown accustomed to such pleasures—very much so. One of his dreams was for a cartoonist to draw a caricature of him. To make the prospective cartoonist's job easier, he made sure he dressed consistently and curled his lower lip in a particular way. Now, when he rose to political stardom and became a worthy subject for a cartoon, the cartoonist would know what to highlight in his drawing!

But then—alas!—India gained her independence, and all his dreams were snatched away. It felt like he had been picked up and cast aside without warning while he was still in the middle of a fiery speech on a public stage. Suddenly one morning, he and the other freedom fighters like him had awakened to the new reality that they were ordinary subjects just like everyone else. People seemed lost, like they had been robbed of something, yet they could not tell what it was, so they wandered aimlessly. Nobody could figure out how to reinvent themselves. Dhamu felt that life had come to a standstill. What was he to do with the tongue that still longed to lash out with fiery speeches? Even his own wife wouldn't applaud him. Not even if he bribed her.

Dhamu adopted the views of a hardline socialist. This seemed a way for him to retain some of his critical approach as well as the culture of protest. Even though India had attained independence, there was more work to be completed, he said. He now spoke in a tone of concern and urgency, as if the immense task of preparing the nation for the revolution was now on his shoulders. But as time passed, he realized that none of it made a mark, and nothing ever made a difference. He grew listless and, finding no other means of escape, fell back on his business. This made his brother Chellappan very happy, and the business thrived under their combined attention. They made money, and for a long while after that Dhamu stayed behind the cash counter, concentrating on the shop. Later, when the Betel Merchants' Association was started, he became a secretary at his friends' insistence. Long after he immersed himself completely in his business, long after he realized that the pleasure of slowly accumulating wealth was no worse than other pleasures, he still sometimes reminisced about those good old days of fame and recognition. He was overcome with self-pity in those moments. He'd say to anyone who happened to be standing nearby: "Politics is in a state of ruin these days. Not so in the old days! It had a certain prestige, you know . . ." It was his way of consoling himself.

Dhamu never expected a return of his glory days. It was all sheer luck. "Not just one black-marketeer like Khader—I will drag a thousand of them out in the open," Dhamu roared on the municipal grounds. It was true that the new circumstances demanded such a tone. But when Dhamu had come out on bail, he had not in the least expected that he would be greeted and garlanded by nearly five hundred merchants. He was deeply moved by it. It felt like Mother India was showing him kindness and calling out to him, "Come, my son, come back to me." He was overcome with emotion.

Even his friends, who were his most ardent fans, felt there was an air of madness to his speech that day. It was true that he went a bit over the top, but it had been so long since he had thundered away like that! For instance, there was no need for him to touch upon the issues of the manual scavengers. Nevertheless, he declared that if the municipality continued to alienate the scavengers, Chairman M. C. Joseph might lose the upcoming election and give up his chair to Comrade Madasami. Many felt that he need not have named names when he spoke of the atrocities perpetrated by business owners. He claimed to have information about the secret warehouses owned by a hundred merchants and demanded to know if the police department was ready to investigate. He sounded a warning to Nehruji, who, he said, gave everyone the impression he was a socialist but was in fact in cahoots with the right wing. Nehruji's downfall was imminent, he said. When he asked any Criminal Investigation Department (CID) officers who might be present at the rally to take careful notes of his last point and pass it along to their superiors, the crowd erupted in applause. I was one of the people who listened to the entirety of his speech that day, and I remember the words "death knell" coming up quite often.

Dhamu's day had indeed returned.

He was in the golden period of his life. He was amazed by how fast the money poured in once he took over the cigarette agency. When the agency was transferred to his name, he heard that a few betel merchants—friends of his, in fact—were muttering behind his back. Indeed, he expected that he would be criticized for turning on Khader, that people would say he did it out of pure self-interest. But the arrest made him a hero who had exposed the black market. So all the grumbles and murmurs faded away.

Celebrations in Dhamu's honor were held in various locations, and the *Travancore Nesan* covered these events in depth. Many people started to say that Dhamu might run in the upcoming municipal elections and that he could win the chairmanship easily. It was also rumored that Madasami might contest in the elections at the ward level.

13.

It was only ten o'clock in the morning, but it was already terribly hot. Women had barely stepped out of their houses before all their painstaking efforts to look beautiful were ruined; they wilted as they might have at the end of a hard workday.

The morning bell had already rung at the local schools and colleges, so the streets found a brief respite from the usual hustle and bustle. A temporary desolation had crept over the town. Boys and girls who were late for school were rushing as fast as they could. The girls looked like they might burst into tears.

Isakki, the journalist, was coming down College Road toward the clock-tower junction. He acted like he was out on a stroll in the moonlight. He had a jaunty rhythm to his gait, and he stopped quite frequently to say hello to people and chat with them. Genially, he pulled aside a few passersby for a chat, and he laughed loudly and heartily. It was clear that he was not on one of his expeditious missions to gather precious bits of news. Usually, he was in a hurry, and it was the kind of hurry only to impress others. The way he saw it, it was all part of the esteem that he accrued as a newspaper reporter. So moments such as these, when he wafted into town like a gentle breeze, were very rare indeed. He considered himself not only a journalist but also an artist, so he knew how important it was to set aside time in the middle of a demanding day to prepare himself to be a creative writer in the future. He often told his fans and the young writers who came to meet him that, sometimes, unique perspectives occurred to him on these strolls and unique sights caught his eye, all of which then led to the dawning of many unique ideas. He also told his readers that his next project would be his greatest creation, but they were never going to read it, because he was sure that it would be banned the moment it was printed. It was sure to make headlines and lead to serious debates in the legislative assembly. No doubt, it would be a terrible headache for the authorities and for the politicians too. But these things cannot be avoided. You cannot fire a gun and expect a piece of cotton to come flying out—it has to be a bullet.

Isakki's clothes had come back from the laundry that morning. For two days, he had had to step out wearing rumpled and somewhat soiled clothes. But today, as if to make up for it, he left home in clean white khaddar clothes. His creative spirit came alive on the days his laundry was returned. On such days, he was an artist wandering around town. So saying that the arrival of his laundry led to his stroll that day is like saying two plus two equals four.

He was thin, skeletal, all skin and bones. His face looked like a bicycle seat, wide skull tapering into a pointed jaw. His eyes, sunken in the deep hollows of his face, could be disturbing at first sight. They looked like someone had taken a chisel and gouged out two hollows where eyes should have been. When he laughed, his eyes completely disappeared into their sockets. And since he laughed a great deal, both genuinely and in pretense, it was quite rare to see his eyes at all.

He was wearing a Kerala-style jibba, with three lines of stitches down the sides. It hung very loose on him. He had tied a kerchief around his neck, and the knot was nestled in the hollow at the base of his throat. In his hands, he carried a black shoulder bag and the day's copy of the *Travancore Nesan*.

As he passed by Excelsior Press, he saw the proprietor, Francis, standing on the steps outside. Isakki greeted him with utmost respect, bringing his palms together in front of his forehead.

"Ah, it's you! Come, come!" said Francis.

"I just remembered something the moment I saw you," Isakki began. "I have a favor to ask of you."

"All that can wait," said Francis. "There was an ad for my press printed in your newspaper yesterday. What are you up to, Isakki? Are you playing games with me?" He grabbed Isakki's right arm and twisted it behind his back.

Isakki quickly turned his back toward Francis to keep his shoulder from dislocating. "Brother, brother, let go of my arm! I can explain. Aah! Aah! It hurts too much . . ."

Francis relaxed his hold a little. Isakki twisted his head over his shoulder and begged, "Brother, please let go of my arm. I will explain." When Francis let go of him, Isakki rubbed his shoulder ruefully. "I was the one who ran the ad, brother," Isakki said. "I heard yesterday that the other guy was planning to start a press. So I thought if you had some publicity right now, it will give you a bit of a boost . . . Do you understand?"

"Who is starting a press?"

"Michael, the one who broke away from you."

"Hey! Why are you so concerned about me? You worry about me like you are my mother! You are going to waste away if you take on all the worries of the town . . ."

"Brother, you have always had a special place in my heart. I swear," said Isakki, placing his right hand on top of Francis's head.

"Now, look here. Go straight to that guy Michael and tell him, 'Your ex-boss got all rattled when he found out you were opening a press,' and get him to print an ad too."

"*Chee! Chee!* That's a cheap thing to do."

"Exactly!"

"I don't have it in me to even think of such a thing, big brother!" said Isakki, dramatically lifting his right hand in a solemn gesture.

"What's wrong with your hand? Do you have eczema? Ooh, is your skin covered in welts? You need to rub some soap-nut powder and oil . . . Let me see your fingers . . ."

"Stop teasing me, brother. I really do need a favor from you. Please give me one-eighth of a pound of the letter K."

"K?! One-eighth of a pound?! What for?"

"I am going to give it back to him good today!"

"Who?"

"The education minister. I think he is going about it all wrong. He will ruin the schoolkids' lives."

"So?"

"So I have to type 'kalvi' [education] a lot, don't I? I am running low on Ks."

"I hope you have enough dots to put above the I. Otherwise, you'll end up printing 'kalavi' [sex] instead of 'kalvi.' Although, it's not going to be the end of the world if you print 'sex' instead of 'education' after all!"

Isakki burst into the most animated laughter, as if he didn't care who was watching. It was also his way of making sure they were done talking about the advertisement.

One of the boys who worked at the press walked in with a coffee in one hand and a parcel of food in the other.

"Brother, nothing for me?" asked Isakki, licking his lips.

"Come on in," said Francis, putting his arms around him and inviting him into the press.

"No, no, actually, I am quite full. Thank you! I need to get going," said Isakki, releasing himself from Francis's affectionate hold.

He arrived at the clock-tower junction, nodding at each merchant sitting at the cashbox of every store along the way. He stopped at a turn at the junction and examined the covers of the magazines hanging at the newsstands. "Sleazy bastards! Making money printing dirty pictures of women? Just you wait. I will sort you out. I'll make your life miserable," he muttered. Then he walked toward the storefront and, with an air of entitlement, picked up an English newspaper and scanned the front page casually, like he was checking to see if they had come even close to printing the things he wrote for them correctly.

Just then, two little boys in shorts arrived at the store to buy a copy of the children's magazine *The Little Mouse*. But they forgot what they had come for and instead stood staring at Isakki. He took the look of surprise on their faces to mean he had been recognized. He knitted his brows to show that he could not care less, turned to the editorial page, and gave it a quick glance from top to bottom. He frowned even more and then folded the paper carelessly and in an exaggerated huff. The newsagent reached out and took the paper from him, refolded it neatly for sale, and smiled at Isakki.

"These fellows have no substance in their lead articles, brother. It's all nonsense! Even their English is bad!" Isakki said, and smiled good-naturedly at the little boys in front of him. They snapped out of their reverie and, with timid smiles, handed over their money and walked away with their magazine.

Isakki left the clock tower and walked through the bazaar toward the tamarind-tree junction. He felt a sudden urge to stop by Dhamu's shop. He could find out the latest developments, learn what new serpents were surfacing and from where. When he reached the tamarind tree, he stood, half hidden behind the tree, and observed Dhamu's shop for a little while. The place was packed. There was a crowd of bicycles parked outside. He surmised it was the day for cigarette distribution. He spotted Chellappan standing next to the steel safe. He was wearing a golden khaddar silk shirt and was smoking a cheroot. "Look at that! Someone's doing well," Isakki muttered to himself.

Dhamu didn't seem to be around, which disappointed Isakki. He couldn't decide where to go next, so he stood looking around aimlessly for a bit. And his eyes landed, by chance, on Khader's store. There was not a soul there. A man sat hunched in a corner, writing accounts. The place looked old and lackluster, as if dusk had cast its darkness over the store. Who knows what thoughts passed through Isakki's mind at that moment? He slowly walked toward Khader's store.

"Brother, how are things? Are you well?" he asked loudly and in a solicitous tone.

The way the bookkeeper raised his head and looked at him had that quality of a machine's first movement.

"I am all right. Same old, same old. No good and bad days for this donkey."

Laughing at the remark, Isakki asked him, "Is the boss here?"

The bookkeeper didn't say anything in reply. Instead, he simply jerked his head toward the ladder.

"Upstairs?"

"Yes."

"Sleeping?"

"At midday?! No. Why would he sleep at this hour? It will stir up the bile."

"He really keeps to himself these days, doesn't he?"

"Well, when you have fallen out of grace, that's the end of you, man . . . You got any snuff?"

Isakki pulled a packet out of his left pocket and offered it to him.

"We can do something to bring some good cheer, *annachi*. Don't worry."

"Cheer up who?"

"The boss."

"And here I thought you were talking about me!"

"It's not hard to cheer you up!"

"Hey, Isakki, you know that old widow who comes from Navakkadu? The one with the huge car?"

"Yes . . ."

"I hear she is worth ten lakhs! And they say she has no kids! Why don't you ask her to adopt me? Come on."

"All right. I'll see what I can do!" Isakki laughed.

"Isakki, do you know the price of okra in the market today? An anna a piece! And look, they are as small as my little finger. You know that Nadar with the topknot? The one who looks like a weasel and sits there in the south corner of the market? He's the one charging that much for okra. Hey, Isakki, you should write about him in your paper, tear him to pieces. I want to kill him. One anna for a piece of okra the size of my little finger! I hope he rots."

"Why not, brother? I can write. I take on people a lot bigger than him . . . Now, let me have a quick word with your boss."

"Hey, wait! What's going on? You never come here. Why do you want to see him today? What's your agenda?"

"No agenda. I just want to talk to him . . ."

"No agenda! That's not possible. You don't work like that! In fact, none of you journalists would know what that even means. I've known your grandpa from the time he was learning his ABCs."

Isakki laughed and walked over to the ladder. The bookkeeper watched him until he disappeared up the rungs, then sniffed a pinch of snuff he had been holding, shook his fingers clean, and returned to his accounts. "Well, the tortoise has entered. That's the end of it, then," he said to himself, referring to Isakki as an ill omen.

Khader was sitting in his easy chair, lost in thought. *"Annachi, vanakkam,"* Isakki said, his palms together and raised high; he stood like that for half a minute, his eyes closed like he was in the thrall of some divine presence.

Isakki's sudden arrival startled Khader; he said, "Come in, come in," and offered Isakki the metal folding chair that had been leaning against the wall.

Isakki took a seat.

Neither of them knew how to start, so they sat there in silence for a minute.

Isakki broke the silence. He looked at Khader's face for a few seconds, then said, "What's happened to you? You've lost a lot of weight!"

"I have not been feeling well for some days now. I get this fever every evening . . ." Khader started saying, but Isakki didn't let him finish.

"You cannot let it all affect you so much. Don't lose heart. This is madness . . ."

"No, no, nothing like that! Nothing terrible has happened to me. Everything's going fine . . ."

"Did you sell the car?"

"Yes. But it was an old vehicle. I couldn't keep up with the repairs. I've ordered a new one. It'll be here in a few months."

"Brother, I want to tell you something. Please don't take it the wrong way. And don't think a young man is giving you advice. Whatever's happening right now is just bad luck. The guy up there is rolling the dice, and none of us down here has any idea what's going to show up for us."

"True enough."

"I've seen them myself. The brothers. They used to buy things in the market and then carry it all home themselves, because they could not even afford a coolie . . ."

"Who are you talking about?"

"Him. Who else? Well, let's say I am talking about a friend of ours. Now, nobody's saying people should know their place and that's where they belong. But still, there's got to be some limits, brother. Just because they've made a little money, they shouldn't imagine they are Maharaja Moolam Thirunal."

"Who are you talking about?"

"Why do you keep asking who I'm talking about! About our next municipal chairman, that's who!"

"Who?"

"Oh! Looks like you haven't heard the news. Don't you read the *Nesan*?"

Isakki took out his newspaper and placed it open in front of Khader.

Khader picked up the paper. The first thing he saw was Dhamu's picture. He read the report.

"So he is contesting in the elections? Somebody did mention it a few days ago."

"We've been hearing about it for ten days now. I didn't believe it at first. Then he showed up at my office yesterday and told me he had filed his nomination and that he was counting on our support . . ."

"Let him contest, let him win, let him become the chairman," said Khader.

"Yes, let him shine! I don't have a problem with that."

"And you give him the support he wants. As it is, your newspaper is all about Dhamu these days. And when people think of Dhamu, they think of your newspaper. So we know how things will be in the future."

"Who? Us?"

"Yes, you. I know what's going on. You print his picture, you publish his speeches, you say he challenged someone or the other, you print headlines that say 'He raised a war cry' against this or that . . . Carry on! What's he paying you for the publicity? A thousand a month?"

" . . ."

"What? No reply?"

"I'll take leave, brother." Isakki rose from his chair and brought his hands together to bid goodbye.

"Why are you leaving so suddenly?"

"Nothing. I can see that you are upset right now. I can easily talk back to you, but I don't want to risk others hearing it. You have the wrong impression of things. I don't know what to say to you."

"Why? Was I wrong in what I said?"

"No, I am not saying you are wrong. You are saying it the way you see it. I just have one thing to say . . ."

"If you think I am wrong, you can set me right," Khader said softly.

151

Isakki sank back into the chair. "You just spat out whatever came to your mind," he said gently. "Let me tell you just one thing. Do you see this pen? This pen is not for sale. Not even for the Nizam of Hyderabad. However, I agree that a newspaper has to whore itself out a bit. I don't deny that. But that does not mean . . ." Isakki wanted to make some emphatic point, but he was now at a loss for words.

"*Chee, chee!* That's not what I meant . . ."

"It doesn't matter how you meant it. I guess it's just my fate that I should sit here and listen to it."

"What's wrong with you? I was just kidding, and you are taking it so seriously. Come on, this is not fair . . ."

"I can't blame you for thinking what you think. It's all my old boss's fault, but I am the one dealing with the consequences. He died, leaving his newspaper and the press to a stupid bitch who was cleaning his house."

"To the sweeper?"

"Yes, yes! Don't you know the story? I'll tell you, but I will try to keep it clean. He and his wife had a big fight. Then she said, 'All right, old man. I don't give a damn about you. I am going to live with my children,' and she packed up and left for Ceylon. Her children were doing really well over there. After that, this fellow set up a stove right in the press, started making his own kanji, and sat scratching the paper trying to come up with editorials. Then he got this boil . . ."

"Who?"

"The owner. On his back. A massive boil. One day he asked her to apply some medicine on it . . ."

"Asked who?"

"Just keep listening . . . She was sweeping the floor in a corner. Then she propped the broom against the wall and attended to his boil."

Khader gave a little laugh.

Isakki felt encouraged by that.

"Now, once she was done treating the boil, did she really still need to keep her hands on him? Well, she didn't take her hands away. One day I said to Samuel, the printer, 'Samuel, she doesn't seem to take her hands off him.' And pat came his reply: 'Isakki, brother, let me put it this way. She didn't put her hand on him so she could take it off.'"

"How old was he at the time?"

"Just a year or two shy of eighty."

"And she?"

"Fifty, fifty-five."

"So what happened next?"

"What's there to happen? Electricity! The man was totally smitten. It came to a point where if you asked him what to write for the editorial, he'd say, 'I will consult her and get back to you.'"

Khader laughed.

"She is definitely a very lucky woman. The old man died within two years, leaving her the press, the paper, everything!"

"That's some story."

"Story? They should make a movie out of it! You should see our plight, now that we work for her. Even the street dogs have it better. She owns three horse-drawn carriages that she rents out. For three years now, I have been trying to tell her that there is a difference between us journalists and carriage drivers. But it doesn't seem to get through that thick skull of hers. She sees me in the morning and the first thing she says is, 'Hey, you! Did you bring in any adoosement yesterday?'"

"What's that?"

"Ad sales. Advertisement. What we call 'vilambaram' in Tamil. She says, 'You! Are you still wasting precious space writing about these loafers who amount to nothing? You need to bring in more adoosement!' . . . Khader, brother, it is a struggle working for her . . . God! . . . But then, I get yelled at by her, then I step outside, and I run into people who tell me things like: 'Hey! You really gave it to Russia in that article!' Or 'You smashed Churchill's head with that one,' or 'You really ripped apart the budget' . . . I feel happy when I hear these things . . . Just a small happiness . . . I mean, I have chosen this life . . . You know what I mean? . . . So what can I do, it's a dog's life . . . I think I will start crying if I carry on . . ."

Khader looked at Isakki's face for a minute or so. What he saw was the face of an innocent child and the face of a master comedian. He felt the urge to laugh, but he also felt pity for the man.

"Dig deep into anybody's life, and it is misery all the way down. What can we do about it? We struggle, but without ever getting to know why the hell we struggle so much. Something is pressing down on our hearts, doesn't even let us laugh. We are in agony because we don't know how to escape that. The more we desire to be aloof and happy, the more we seem to get mired in this muck and keep sinking . . . ," said Khader.

"*Annachi*, you might disagree with me here, but this is what I have arrived at. People keep saying that the Tirukkural says this, the Gita says that, that the answer is in the Bible, that there's nothing to beat the Koran . . . But none of it is of any use for people like us. Nothing but pain from the moment we are born. Nothing but struggle. Every single day is a torment . . ."

"You are absolutely right."

The conversation had worn itself out.

Khader leaned back on his chair and looked out the window. Isakki sat still, staring at the floor.

After a few minutes, Khader asked, "Are you upset with me?"

Isakki looked up at Khader and smiled. "No, no! Not at all. I was thinking about something else."

"I didn't mean to hurt your feelings . . ."

"Don't worry about it! Just let it go. I've already forgotten about it. Besides, you've got every right to correct me. Every right. You can even twist my ear and say to me, '*Thambi*, you are going down the wrong path. Do the right thing.' Now, no matter what you think of me, I am going to tell you what I came to tell you . . ." Isakki took out the packet of snuff from his pocket. Turning his face away from Khader, he took a sniff and stared at the opposite wall until his face regained its composure after all its contortions. Then he snapped his head back to Khader and said, "Brother, this is a good chance for you."

Khader looked at Isakki without asking what he meant.

"Shall I tell you?"

"Sure."

"I don't say this lightly. I have given it some thought, and I think this is your chance. I hear he is contesting from the Thirteenth Ward. Do you know how many votes your people have in that ward?"

Khader said nothing.

Isakki pulled out a piece of paper from his shirt pocket.

"Over seven hundred votes, *annachi*. Out of the total votes of two thousand or so, you Muslims have got seven hundred. At least. If you get somebody from Dhamu's caste to contest, then we can also split those votes and you can beat him easily. You don't have to worry about anything. I will speak to our friend Chairman M. C. Joseph and take care of everything. He is filthy rich. This is nothing for him. If he decides not to deposit his estate income in the bank this year, everything will come to a grinding halt. We worry about just one Dhamu. Joseph can throw ten Dhamus into the sea in Kanyakumari! That boy has no idea whom he is messing with . . ."

"Wait . . . What's Chairman M. C. Joseph got to do with any of this? Why drag him into this?"

"*Annachi*, don't you see what's going on? Didn't I tell you? Dhamu's plan is not just to become a mere councilman. He wants to become the municipal chairman! So he is coming for M. C. Joseph's job! So Joseph is thinking about fronting a promising candidate against Dhamu and putting his weight behind him. He wants to nip this in the bud . . ."

"Oh! I see."

"That's the reason I am telling you all this in confidence. The truth is, unless Dhamu is taken down, he will make life difficult for everyone in this town."

"He is arrogant because he's got some money now."

"It's all from this new business, right? He thinks no one can throw a wrench in that. If I set my mind to it, I can make sure Dhamu starts losing money within twenty-four hours! His earnings will get slashed in half. That should put him in his place. If that does not work, I can always pull out the big guns. I've already got a plan . . . but no point telling you about it now, though. You can't get it done on your own. Not just you in particular. Everyone's scared of him now. I mean, I agree he is a total thug, but you all have turned him into a big man by being so scared of him!"

"Me?" Khader said. "Why would I be afraid of that stupid dog? I've known three generations of that family. His grandmother worked in the maharaja's palace. Her job was to make beds. I know how his people made their living! They pimped out all their pretty girls to any royal men they could find. If you ask him his father's name, he'll give you a different one every week. Why the hell would I be scared of such a man?!"

"No need to dig into that sewer, *annachi*! No need at all to dig into that wide, wide sewer," said Isakki, holding his nose.

"Well, you were the one making a big deal about it!"

"No, brother. I am not making a big deal of it. I am just sick and tired of everyone's behavior. They stand up the moment they see him, they make sure their veshtis are not folded in his presence, they salute to him, they keep calling him 'our leader' . . . These stupid bastards are out of control."

"See, wherever there's a butcher shop, there will always be a few stray dogs sniffing around. There's nothing we can do about it."

"But he has us over the barrel, *annachi*! Let's say I go over there tomorrow and chop down the tamarind tree. What will he do about it? Tell me," asked Isakki.

"Chop down the tamarind tree? What are you talking about! He will be glad about it. There'll be fewer leaves on the ground. He'll have to sweep in front of the store only once, in the morning. He will be happy he won't have to sweep again at dusk."

"But his cashbox will be empty, *annachi*! His cashbox will be empty!"

"You are not making any sense."

"Oh, I am making perfect sense. I have thought about this, *annachi*. His business does not depend on the actual items he sells. You can find the same stuff in a hundred shops around here. His business relies on the shade of the tree. If we take away the shade, his business will collapse. No doubts about that."

Khader fell silent, staring intently at Isakki. This silence was all the encouragement Isakki needed.

"It's a very subtle idea, *annachi*. Takes some brains to grasp it."

"I see your point, but I don't think it will have such a huge impact."

"It will! Without a doubt. See, your shop is different. The customers can step in. There, at Dhamu's, people can't go into the shop. They have to stand outside on the steps the entire time they are buying things. Right now, it's the shade that makes people want to linger even when they are done with their purchases. It coaxes them to buy and eat a few bananas. It makes them chew some betel or smoke a cigarette. So if there is no shade, it will affect everything. Not just a small impact. It will cut him to the bone."

"Let's say you are right about this. What can you do about it? You need an axe to chop down that tree, and all you've got is that old pen of yours! You will break the nib if you stab the tree with it . . ."

Isakki laughed. "That's true. You do need an axe for the job. And the one swinging the axe needs to carry an official order. And *that* order should carry the municipal chairman's signature. You are right about that. But this cracked old pen I hold in my hand? All it needs to do is to fill up a few blank pages with writing. Then, one fine morning, on your way to open the store, you will see the tamarind tree going away in the back of a lorry . . ."

"Hear! Hear!" said Khader.

"This is no empty talk. I have already sown the seeds in the right places. Now all I need to do is to keep watering them from time to time. When they start putting out leaves, goats will come for a bite; those opportunists need to be driven away. But there is something I need to take care of first. That's why I came to this part of town today. But he is not around . . ."

"Who?"

Isakki looked Khader in the eye with a furtive expression on his face. He shot a quick glance toward the ladder and looked back at Khader. Then he dragged his chair closer and leaned in.

"I wanted to see Dhamu today. There's something I need to discuss with him in private . . ."

"Oh, really?"

"Here's the thing. M. C. Joseph sent for me yesterday out of the blue. It was two at night. His brother-in-law came over in a jeep and told me Joseph wanted to see me right away. What could I do? How could I refuse? Joseph's been like a brother to me. He's done me some huge favors. Of course, I have done him some favors too. But it's not about that. This is about our affection for each other. He feels better when he discusses things with me. So I went. And there he was, wide awake, out on the front porch and pacing like a bear! He told me what the matter was. I asked him just one thing: '*Annachi*, don't you think it is insulting to me that you will be in so much anguish over such a small thing?' He said, 'No, it's not like that. He is a tough guy, and I hear he has made some money recently, so he's now got some influence too.' I got so mad at that! 'So? What do you propose to do? Do you want to declare bankruptcy and put on a loincloth?' Those were my exact words. Joseph hemmed and hawed. So I asked him, 'You are seated on top of an elephant. Why are you so scared about a barking dog?' Then he said, 'All right, all right. I won't worry about this. Now that you have reassured me, I won't let it bother me. You'll see, I will be brave.' Then

I thought, I'll speak to Dhamu and make sure I sort things out. That's why I came here today . . ."

"And you couldn't see Dhamu? He's usually at the store by now."

"This is all I want to tell him: 'Look, assembly elections are coming up six months from now. We can get you a ticket there, and we can definitely make you win. But if you cross Chairman M. C. Joseph now, then you won't find even a single ballot in your name, not even if you turn the ballot box upside down and give it a vigorous shake. So be a good boy now and withdraw your nomination for the municipal elections.' I am going to have to be firm with him."

"What if he says no?"

"The pen in my hand will take care of things. Someone once asked Napoleon which was mightier, the pen or the sword—"

Khader waved his hand impatiently. "Forget these old stories, Isakki. We need to focus on what we need to do now."

Isakki refocused. "All it takes is a few choice headlines," he said. "He'll be ruined."

"Well . . . we'll see who is ruined. Him or M. C. Joseph."

"The only way Joseph will be finished is if I die of a heart attack today!"

"Don't get angry. I am asking you out of ignorance. What can you really do to him?"

"Nothing. I can't slash his throat, can I? Can I break his arms and legs? No. But I can make him eat dirt. That's all I can do."

"So you will make him eat dirt! What, you plan to sneak up behind him and give him a push?"

"Fine, we don't have to argue about this now. You'll see when they count the votes."

"So you really think he will withdraw?"

"I can't say for sure. It all depends on whether he is smart or stupid."

"I'll tell you one thing. I have known him for fifteen years now. Once he sets his mind on something, he gets it done . . ."

"Let him try!"

"Why are you so concerned about Chairman M. C. Joseph?"

"I told you. He's been like a brother to me. And as people come, he is solid gold. But there's more. Who do you think Joseph is? He is my old boss's younger brother . . ."

"His own brother?"

"Same father, different mothers. He is the son of the youngest wife."

"Ah! So that's it."

"So the lady says to me today . . ."

"What lady?"

"The one who owns my paper. She said to me this morning, 'Young man, my brother-in-law needs to win this election. Keep that in mind when you write. OK? Stop writing nonsense. This is a matter of family honor now . . .'"

"Oh, there is such a thing, I suppose . . ."

"She talks like they have been related for thousands of years, you know!"

"So your veshti is folded up and you are in the fray now."

"Yes, yes, yes! There's no doubt about that. You please think over what I told you . . ."

"Think over what?"

"What I just told you. Go and file your candidacy. We'll make sure you win. I'll bring Joseph *annachi* over to your place one day. We can discuss further then."

"But I am going to need some time to think this over . . ."

"Of course. This is no small matter. Think it over carefully. We have a week's time . . . Anyway, I'll get going now. The time flies when I stop to chat with you . . . See you later!"

Khader watched Isakki leave. Then he leaned back into his easy chair and closed his eyes.

14.

Khader's decision to contest in the elections was published in the *Travancore Nesan*. The newspaper printed Khader's picture just as it had printed Dhamu's, which people considered evidence of its impartiality. They were not surprised, therefore, when the *Travancore Nesan* published an editorial ruthlessly attacking Dhamu and urging every self-respecting citizen of the Thirteenth Ward to cast their votes for Khader. In their opinion, the *Nesan* was simply continuing its impeccable service to the community. They gossiped about the editorials that were to follow, eager to see how the paper would rip Dhamu apart. Everyone knew that once Isakki began digging into a sewer, he dug wide and deep—he always did a thorough job, our Isakki. So they were quite hopeful.

The election grew to a feverish pitch. As expected, it grew more intense each day. There were impassioned speeches, attacks, counterattacks. Local firebrands cried themselves hoarse and ruined their throats at rallies, but they pushed through the strain until, eventually, their throats had to relent and open up. After that, they were unstoppable. Political leaflets circulated with no mention of the publisher's name on them. Green, red, purple, light green, pink, violet . . . so many colors! The kids had a great time. They collected as many leaflets as they could, stuffing them into their bags and showing off their collections to each other with pride. Speakers now pounded their fists on the podium. Women, who were usually stuck inside their homes for most of the day and bored, now simply had to step out onto their front steps to witness the spectacle of the political rally. They quite enjoyed watching the podium-pounding. The streets of the Thirteenth Ward were abuzz with activity. There was always something new to hear and discuss. Even the habitually lazy were now caught up in the excitement.

Dhamu was definitely shaken up by Khader's decision to contest, but he kept it to himself. There were a considerable number of Muslim votes in that constituency. Votes from the Vellala community came next, split into two blocs, the patrilineal and matrilineal groups. The matrilineal one was split into five subgroups and the patrilineal into three. In Dhamu's tentative calculation, if everything worked out fine, he could count on considerable votes from most of these groups. People from one of the patrilineal groups were saying that they would rather vote for a Muslim than for someone from their rival matrilineal community, but then they felt that nothing justified voting for a Muslim, so they might as well not vote at all. Apparently, one young lad objected to this, and said, "It's an unforgivable sin not to vote in a democracy!" To which an elder had replied, "Yeah? What's it to you? Mind your own business!" All this was reported in the *Nesan* by one "Town Sparrow."

The truth was that Dhamu had decided to contest in the elections only because he could count on the Muslim votes. His friends had promised him this. Khader's entry into the race was utterly unexpected, and now Dhamu feared he might lose a considerable percentage of the Muslim votes. But his Muslim friends were steadfast in their support of Dhamu. They told him that the only hurdle Khader's entry had created was that they could no longer canvas openly for Dhamu as they'd originally planned, but they would still zealously work for him behind the scenes. They also warned him that he should expect to lose some of the women's votes to communal loyalties.

At the last minute, Dhamu's friends and his brother Chellappan came up with a brilliant plan.

There was a madrassa in the Thirteenth Ward, in front of which an elderly Muslim man sold peanuts, puffed rice, chewy candy, and such. He'd been sitting at that spot for over twenty-five years. He had been a tailor before his eyesight failed him and now he sold candy to survive. The children affectionately called him Grandpa Peanut.

One fine morning, when Grandpa Peanut came out of his hut, everyone who saw him blinked and looked again. They were startled by his appearance. His shirt didn't have a single tear or patch—in fact, it was brand new! A long-sleeved shirt made of excellent fabric. A double-fold veshti around his waist. New boots on his feet. A shiny new red fez on his head. A *car* even pulled up in front of his hut. Grandpa Peanut got into the car with his seven grandchildren, all of whom could not wait to go for a drive. Grandpa Peanut was driven to the municipality office. They only had till 12:00 p.m. that day to declare his candidacy; the clock struck twelve exactly as the old man finished putting his thumbprint on all the forms.

Grandpa Peanut was now contesting in the elections.

With a garland around his neck, he was brought in a procession through the streets. Schoolchildren ran behind the car, wild with joy and yelling, "Peanut *thatha*! Grandpa Peanut!" He picked up as many of the kids as he could in the car. It was an early-model car, a convertible with the top rolled up and secured at the back. The kids clung to the doors and stood on the running boards; some of them even perched on the rolled-up top. The old man was surrounded by children.

Grandpa Peanut was absolutely thrilled, and his face beamed with joy. He smiled at everyone, his toothless mouth wide open behind his beard like a mouse hole under a bush. He pressed his hands together and greeted everyone on the way. His kids were absolutely delighted.

The kids from the madrassa, the kids on the street—they were all his children in a way. He was "Grandpa Peanut" to every single one of them, and now he got to take them all for a ride in the car.

Once the car arrived in front of his hut, he tapped the driver on the shoulder and asked him to stop. His granddaughters stood at the entrance, looking at him with great admiration. Dark eyes peered through every hole in the gunnysack curtains that hung from the front doors of the neighborhood huts. Fingers drew the curtains aside for a good look. Half-shielded faces peered out from everywhere. His oldest granddaughter held up her little baby and shouted, "Grandpa! Grandpa!" The old man held out his arms for the baby, a little boy brought the baby to him, and Grandpa Peanut sat the baby on his lap. The procession resumed. The children's delighted shouts made it clear that Grandpa Peanut had secured all their votes.

The procession passed by Khader's house. The front door was closed and the windows shut. But Khader's children had slipped out through the back door and were standing on the front steps.

The old man called out to them, "Hey Khaja, hey Mahmood, hey Ali! Whom are you going to vote for?"

"Grandpa Peanut!" they shouted in unison.

"What about your father?"

"We won't vote for him!"

"Come on, then. Get in the car!"

The three kids didn't even wait for the car door to be opened. They jumped right in through the open top, and the procession resumed.

※

One by one, election promises began to pile up. There was a Sivan temple at the turning toward Pillaimar Street. Its outer wall had collapsed and lay in ruins. Dhamu obtained special permission from the temple board and arranged for the wall to be rebuilt. The work went on day and night. He also distributed free clothes to children from poor Muslim families.

One of Khader's election promises was that he would get a water pump installed on Vellala Street. He said that he could not bear the sight of Hindu women carrying their pots and walking to far-off wells to fetch water.

Khader's father-in-law, Aziz, arrived from Kalakkad. Things had by now become strained between him and Khader. Aziz was convinced that Khader's stupidity was entirely to blame for the loss of the cigarette franchise. When the whole mess had erupted, he had hoped Khader would come to Kalakkad and seek his advice. If that had happened, he could have untangled the mess and impressed Khader with his resourcefulness. He had even thought up many ideas and fixes. But Khader never gave him the chance to share them, so Aziz began to feel that Khader was disrespecting him by ignoring him, and he constantly spoke ill of Khader to his young wife. He told her his history with Khader, how he had been the first one to give him a break and how Khader seemed to have forgotten everything and become utterly ungrateful. His wife was amazed at how, day after day, he was intent on launching into a tirade against an enemy who was not even there.

Even the news of Khader's contesting in the elections he learned only from reading the newspaper. "I'm sure somebody has put him up to this. Well, he's still got that house to lose. Once that happens, he'll really be out on the street," said Aziz. He started railing against Khader to all his friends. "There's no mystery to this. The boy has decided he wants to go back to rolling beedis! That's all there is to it."

Nevertheless, he started waking up at dawn so he could get to the market and wait for the bus that brought the morning newspapers. In addition to reading the dailies, he also managed to drag the latest information from passengers who got off the bus.

The news of Grandpa Peanut's candidacy made his stomach turn. "This bastard's got in the way now!" he muttered. It came as a serious blow to his secret hope that Khader would win. But since he had ranted so much against Khader to his wife, he couldn't bring himself to share his true concerns with her now. So he gave her some lame excuse and boarded a bus.

The bus entered town, and Aziz started counting the election posters on the walls to see who had more, his son-in-law or his opponents. Once he got off the bus, he booked a room and left his suitcase there, then headed straight to Grandpa Peanut's hut. But he didn't expect such stubbornness from the old man.

"Look here, Aziz," said the old man. "I am not going to drop out even if you give me one lakh gold coins."

"Then you are going to let the other man win."

"Well, as far as I am concerned, your son-in-law is an 'other man' too! Ten years ago, I owed less than ten rupees for a pair of lungis I bought in his store. He had his lawyers send me a collection notice! Did he think of me as a fellow Muslim then? So don't waste your breath, Aziz. Money's the only thing that matters to people. Rich people always band together; it doesn't matter what caste they are from and what gods they worship. If you are so keen that one of our people should win, then why don't you ask your son-in-law to drop out? How does that sound?"

"I am going to make sure you lose. That's my only goal now," said Aziz.

"That's not going to happen. So go mind your own business," the old man said.

"I don't even care if Dhamu wins. I want you to lose."

"Then come to the municipal office on the first of next month. You will see me sitting under the ceiling fan! Then you can rip your tongue out and die!" yelled Grandpa Peanut.

Things got out of hand. The old man started shouting like a man possessed. His eyes went red, and veins popped out on his neck. The women in the hut began screaming. Children came running, gathered around, and raised such a ruckus that Aziz could not get a word in. One of the kids knocked off Aziz's cap from behind. When he bent down to pick it up, someone else pulled his shawl off his shoulders and threw it in the air.

Aziz got out of there as fast as he could. The children chased him down the street, hooting and hollering and yelling inventive insults.

15.

Despite intense opposition, the motion to cut down the tamarind tree passed by a margin of three votes in the municipal council. The *Travancore Nesan* gave this news a six-column headline on its front page. There was also an editorial that praised the municipal chairman M. C. Joseph to the skies.

I still remember the commotion that broke out the day the news was published.

People gathered everywhere—at the Vadaseri market, all around the clock tower, in the bazaar at the tamarind-tree junction, and in Kambolam in Kottar—to discuss the development. The overwhelming opinion was that Dhamu's opposition to the motion to cut the tree down had suffered a great defeat. Many felt the decision was going to have an indirect impact on his election chances. Others spoke of how excited Khader and his minions would be by this development. They imagined how Khader's camp would now throw itself into the campaign with gusto. Listening to them talk, it seemed they had conjured up an entire imaginary scene of war, with Khader's army advancing with great force and Dhamu's army, which had hitherto fought tirelessly, now beating a hasty retreat.

The *Travancore Nesan* found an enduring place in the holy pedestals of its readers' minds. I lost count of the people who said of Isakki, "Now that's a man born to wield the pen!" In a way, he was indeed deserving of these praises. Who could now question his ability to use his pen to make everyone think?

For credit goes to Isakki—and Isakki alone—for creating an entire popular movement with his pen. It was he who first demanded that the municipality cut down the tamarind tree. He advanced so many compelling reasons for it! Like a trained student of history, he analyzed the tree's long past. God only knows where he dug up those old stories from! He wrote as if the tamarind tree had told him its own story from the time it had just sprouted a few leaves all the way up to the present day. Or else, he might have conferred with our beloved, long-dead Damodara Asan!

He wrote that the tamarind tree was a harbinger of bad luck. That it was cursed. An inauspicious omen. How beautifully he wrote that old story of Chellathayi's suicide by hanging on that tree, adding his own new flourishes to the narrative! He brought a new perspective to an old story, arguing that the rotting of the dried-out leaves and withered branches that fell into the pond had made it reek so badly that it ruined Maharaja Pooram Tirunal's procession.

He exposed a secret that had not come to people's attention in all these years. When the tamarind pond was filled in and the new road was laid, he wrote, the British engineer in charge of that project said in his original submission that the tamarind tree needed to be cut down, but some miscreants had intervened at the last minute and stopped it from happening. Isakki demanded to know which power in the world would offer just compensation if a branch from the decrepit old tree were to fall on the head of a little girl from a poor family walking back home from school. He beseeched every compassionate human being in town to take one look at the crowds that gathered beneath the tree, in front of the cinema and the stores, and then imagine what would happen if the tree were to fall on them suddenly.

There were several letters to the editor printed in the *Travancore Nesan*. Many wrote in support of Isakki's proposal. One reader pointed out an old incident in some village in north India where a tree had fallen down and killed many people. Isakki also included the opinions of several eminent scholars, whom he had interviewed in person. Everyone was impressed by the fact that the entire academic community was in unanimous agreement with Isakki's views on the matter.

The chief of the electricity board also wrote in favor of getting rid of the tree. He justified his position by noting that the tamarind tree's branches often brushed against the power lines, interrupting the power supply and plunging the entire town into darkness without any warning. He also added that it was always hazardous to have a living tree at a spot where so many power lines crisscrossed, and that he had long ago given the municipality his professional opinion on the matter. His views and his photo took up half a page.

The implicit conclusion of the report submitted by the committee that the municipal chairman M. C. Joseph had asked Umaiyorubagam Pillai to head, to inquire into the theft of the tamarind harvest, was that they could not find out for sure who did it. But the committee's report said that there was sufficient evidence to surmise that Khader's store sign had been broken when the unidentified vandals threw stones at the tamarind tree that was owned by the municipality, the same municipality that also collected taxes on store signs. Therefore, the report suggested, the best course of action to ensure such unfortunate incidents did not occur in the future would be to cut down the tree.

The report came up for debate in the municipal council. Kambaramayanam Ananthan Pillai was the only person who spoke in vehement opposition. "This town is a holy place, and the tamarind tree is sacred to it," he said. "The tree might be mute, it might also be maimed, but it is still a living thing." He also warned that people who needed no other reason to cut down the tamarind tree besides the fact that it was only a tree might one day also suggest we get rid of the disabled and the maimed. He called them crude materialists. When he cited the work of botanist J. C. Bose to argue that trees were indeed sentient beings, and when he launched into a sweeping rendition of old Tamil poetry to show how the Tamil people had long worshipped the tree as divine, the council marveled at his scientific knowledge and his command of Tamil literature. He ended his speech by saying, "If you are really keen on wiping the mark of auspiciousness off a married woman's forehead, go ahead. May God forgive you."

After debating the matter for two days, the council passed a resolution in support of cutting down the tamarind tree.

Khader was thrilled to read the *Travancore Nesan* that day. He read the full account of the municipal council's debate twice, as well as the council's final resolution in support of cutting down the tree. He was pleased that, in this matter at least, he was able to defeat Dhamu.

The series of election tactics that Dhamu had unleashed caught Khader completely off guard. The craftiness that Dhamu's men had shown in nominating a Muslim candidate against Khader and funding his entire campaign—thus ensuring that the entire Muslim community rallied behind him—had dealt a death blow to Khader's aspirations. When he went door to door seeking votes, it became abundantly clear that the women and the elderly in his constituency were deeply sympathetic to Grandpa Peanut. The old man was familiar to them; he'd been welcome in their homes for years. Besides, the children were pestering the adults nonstop to vote for Grandpa Peanut. Women were saying to the old man, "You have been toiling in the hot sun for so many years. You definitely have our votes and our family's votes, if that's what it takes to get you out of the sun." Khader also found out that the women were making secret gifts of money, paddy, and rice to the old man.

This is what Grandpa Peanut said to them when he went door to door asking for votes: "If you want me to be able to afford the same kind of clothes I am wearing today, if you want me to have a little to eat every day, please cast your votes for me. I am getting on in age, and this will at least get me out of the sun. Khader's still young. If he doesn't win this, he will soon find some other way to thrive." Many elderly women challenged Khader to his face: "Why are you ruining this for the old man? He's struggling to make a living. You expect us to believe you are in the same position?"

Khader encountered some such experience every single day, and it only strengthened his hatred of Dhamu. At one point, he even considered withdrawing his candidacy so he could throw his weight behind the old man and get him to win, if that was what it took to ensure Dhamu's defeat. But his father-in-law had come to have such animosity toward the old man, Khader couldn't bring himself to tell him. He also worried that people would think he had dropped out because he was afraid of the old man, and then he'd be disgraced. Moreover, he had received a lot of campaign money from Chairman M. C. Joseph and had already spent a great deal of it. The money had been given to him with the understanding that he would defeat Dhamu. But since he was in no position to return the money, dropping out now would be unjustifiable; it would amount to defrauding Joseph.

Amid all this, Khader was dealt another blow—the cases filed against Dhamu regarding the store sign were dismissed in court. There were no reliable witnesses who would testify that Dhamu had hired someone to break Khader's store sign. Nor could the police find any witnesses to corroborate their claim that the manual scavengers had thrown stones at the tamarind tree. The scavengers said it was lawyer Janardhanan's brilliance that destroyed the police's case against them. Since the police could not establish that the scavengers had indeed thrown stones at the tree, their other case also fell apart, in which they had argued that Dhamu had taken advantage of that situation to break Khader's store sign because he hoped the blame would fall on the scavengers.

Khader grew dejected at how every single one of his trump cards had slipped away from him. It was around then that the *Travancore Nesan* engineered the crusade to cut down the tree. When Khader read Isakki's article on the tree, he remembered everything Isakki had said to him the day he'd come to see him. Khader still didn't set much store by the secret weapons that Isakki said he possessed against Dhamu. But he felt that Isakki's growing reputation as a political mastermind could mean he did have something up his sleeve. Also, if Khader's fears were to be proven wrong in the end and Dhamu did lose, that would be a most welcome turn of events indeed. So Khader realized it would be a mistake not to cooperate at this point. His final prayer was that, even if the election ended up costing him his social standing and his financial status, Dhamu should also suffer comparable loss.

Khader became one of the main pillars of the campaign to cut down the tamarind tree. A leaflet was published in his name. He began to address the issue in his election rallies.

⋊

Until then, Dhamu had been completely immersed in his election campaign and had paid no attention to the tamarind-tree issue, so he felt uneasy about Khader's new interest in the subject. He suspected that Khader was merely making a show of concern because he was keen on remaining in Isakki's and Chairman M. C. Joseph's good books. But then, one evening, Dhamu learned the truth about the crusade against the tree.

By this time, business at Khader's store had dropped to nothing. The moment he lost the cigarette agency, his cash flow dwindled. But Khader was unwilling to cut down on his personal or domestic expenses. In fact, he spent even more than before, just so others would not think he had fallen on hard times. He was afraid that people would misinterpret something as mundane as his walking down the street, so he took taxis even when he didn't need to. But the truth was that he had no cash left to invest in his business, and his store shelves began to look scanty. He tried his best to rearrange the merchandise so they would look ample, but as days passed by, the shelves looked bare. There was nothing he could do about the situation, so he completely lost interest in his business.

When the elections came up, defeating Dhamu became his sole aim. But when the business ground to a complete halt, he could not keep paying salaries. He had to let a few of his employees go with a cash payout. But he found it impossible to lay off the shop boys who had been very loyal to him. The boys held their breath for a few months, even though he could not pay them their salaries, but once the money owed them grew large enough to affect their basic sustenance, they quietly slipped away and found jobs in other shops. In the end, the only one left was the bookkeeper. Khader requested him to stay on and help settle some outstanding dues, and the man agreed and got busy wrapping up the accounts. Just as he suspected, he could not get a salary from Khader for this work, but he invented a few emergencies to get a little money out of him. Then Dhamu approached him and made a secret offer of a job at his store. Dhamu thought it was an excellent idea to bring in a man who had experience managing accounts at a wholesale cigarette agency. The bookkeeper accepted Dhamu's offer.

It was the bookkeeper who explained to Dhamu why Isakki and Chairman M. C. Joseph had instigated the movement to cut down the tamarind tree, and why Khader had taken such an avid interest in that project. It happened like this: One day, Dhamu went to his store to pick up some cash he needed for election expenses. When he got there, he found his brother Chellappan and his friends engaged in a heated debate about the resolution passed by the municipality.

"I get your point, brother. But why is that Khader fellow so concerned about it all? Why the hell is he so intent on making sure the tree is cut down?" Dhamu asked his brother.

"That guy's a fool," said Chellappan.

"See, right now it is M. C. Joseph who is throwing him the crumbs. So he has to wag his tail toward him a little, doesn't he?" said one of the friends sitting on the bench in front of Chellappan.

The bookkeeper, who had been leaning over the ledger, looked up over his glasses at everybody sitting there and said, "Is it so easy to figure out why assurance money has exchanged hands?" His tone and expression suggested that the matter was more serious than they assumed.

Dhamu studied the bookkeeper's face.

When he became aware of how Dhamu was looking at him, the bookkeeper put on an expression of innocence that was meant to suggest that he was powerless to withstand such scrutiny and that it was all none of his business anyway, and he lowered his head and returned to his ledger.

"Why don't you tell us what you think?" said Dhamu.

The bookkeeper looked up at Dhamu and then scanned the small crowd of people sitting with Chellappan.

"All friends here. Not to worry. Just tell us," said Dhamu.

The bookkeeper now spoke in a low voice. "Well, the way they see it, this is their plan to dig our graves."

"Why would I give a damn whether the tree is cut down or not?" Dhamu asked. "That's not going to affect our livelihood, is it?"

"When the tree goes, so will the shade. That's what they are counting on."

"So?"

"They think this business depends on the shade of the tree. So they figure when the shade goes, our business will fall."

Chellappan burst out laughing.

"I am not saying they are right. I am just telling you what they think. That's all," said the bookkeeper.

Dhamu sat absolutely silent, his face betraying no emotion. After a minute's thought, he stood up and walked into the store. As soon as Dhamu disappeared behind the door to the back room, the bookkeeper jumped up and ran inside, as though Dhamu had signaled him to join him.

Half an hour later, Dhamu left the store and walked over to his campaign office.

The bookkeeper was incredibly pleased with how things had turned out. He had found an excellent opportunity to prove to them that he had no loyalty left to Khader and to demonstrate his total reliance on his new employer's kindness.

At the campaign rally that evening, Dhamu strongly condemned the municipality's resolution to cut down the tamarind tree.

"It looks like you are actually rattled by their plan," Chellappan said to Dhamu that night over dinner. "You got a little carried away tonight. It felt like you actually believe we will be ruined the moment that tree is cut down."

"I don't have that fear at all. Even so, it is clear that they are determined to cut down the tree because they believe that will ruin us. So I think we should take that challenge head-on. Their plan should not succeed. It's another matter entirely what we lose if the tree is indeed cut down."

Dhamu and a few bigwigs in his ward drafted a detailed formal statement, obtained the signatures of hundreds of prominent residents of the ward, and submitted it to the municipal chairman. Dhamu organized a procession, with him in the lead, to carry that statement to the municipal office. Everyone could see Kambaramayanam Ananthan Pillai walking out in front of the crowd with a garland around his neck.

At the municipal office, a huge argument broke out between him and Chairman M. C. Joseph. Dhamu took the chairman's stubbornness about cutting down the tree as a clear sign that the man was indeed at the helm of a conspiracy against him.

"I cannot even begin to explain to you how the Hindus feel about this," said Dhamu. "The tree should not be cut down."

The chairman said: "I admit that I know nothing about the Hindus' particular sentiments about the tree. But at the same time, let me point out to you that this resolution was passed by a council that is majority Hindu."

"Who is a Hindu?" asked Ananthan Pillai. "Those who are born Hindu or those who protect Hindu dharma? Do you realize that Hinduism is a way of life? It's not like Christianity . . . ," he said, raising his voice.

But Chairman M. C. Joseph cut him off. "Excuse me. I am not the right person to get into a debate with about religion. I am nothing but a mere head of an ordinary institution."

"But there are mercenaries in all religions. I hope you know that," said Dhamu.

"That's disgraceful, to refer to municipal employees as mercenaries," said M. C. Joseph.

"How could people who have no standards be disgraced? Show me a law in this country that says that when a man who is involved in illegal trading comes up with a plan to destroy an independent merchant and he's found a corrupt journalist to endorse it, the municipality is duty-bound to see that plan to its conclusion!"

"You may leave now," said M. C. Joseph, and he pressed the bell on his desk. A peon held the door open and stood looking at Dhamu and Ananthan Pillai.

"So I take it that you have no intention to honor our feelings. Am I right?"

"A democratic institution can only honor the feelings of the majority. It's one of the great paradoxes that even people who have no faith in democracy will run for election in our country," said the chairman.

Dhamu and Ananthan Pillai left.

16.

Those days when the tamarind tree was the talk of the town from dawn to dusk are still vivid in my memory. How impassioned people were about the issue! The way they talked about it, you'd think it was their family affair. The issue of the tamarind tree had become the deciding factor in a tug of war between two parties. And everyone in town had their predictions about which party would emerge victorious in the end.

As far as the municipality was concerned, its own honor was at stake in this matter. Everyone—from the municipal council members who were close friends with Chairman M. C. Joseph to employees like Valli who had many years of experience in administration—was of the opinion that if the municipality was cowed by its opponents and failed to carry through on its resolution, it would lose its credibility and its future ability to govern effectively. People were saying that the job of cutting the tree down had been given to a contractor from out of town, that the municipality had written to the Thiruvananthapuram police seeking reinforcements, and that the date for cutting down the tree would be fixed once they heard back from the city police.

While everyone was busy talking about these events, something totally unexpected happened.

One morning, utter pandemonium erupted at the tamarind-tree junction. Apparently, the tamarind tree had become a deity.

As I write this now, I remember how my friends and I ran to the junction as soon as we heard the news and how we stood there, pushed and shoved in that crowd, all sweaty and dizzy in the heat, but utterly spellbound as we took in the scene in front of us.

At the tamarind-tree junction, music from a nadaswaram party jostled with music from a brass band. And if these weren't enough, there were also musicians from a naiyandi melam folk-music group. There was also talk that Agasteeswaram Anantapadmanabha Pillai would be performing villupaattu, a form of musical storytelling, that night on his bow-shaped string instrument.

Rituals for the goddess were in full swing in front of the tamarind tree. A giant heap of oleander, jasmine, and lotus had been piled at the base of the tree. Just above this heap of flowers, a perfect circle of bark had been peeled from the tree and a silver face of the goddess had been set in it. A thick splotch of vermilion had been applied on her forehead, and green stones sparkled in her eyes. Sunlight fell on this image of the goddess and scattered out in thick sparkling bands of light. The air was heavy with the fragrance of incense sticks. Everyone wore a vertical stripe of sandalwood paste on their foreheads. Every pious face in town seemed to have assembled there. There were also several well-known bearded swamis who often headed groups of Ayyappan devotees—after they had taken the vows and worn the beaded garlands—to the temple up in the mountains. Ganapati Iyer from Asiramam was there too, looking majestic, like a Vedic sage. There were many who believed he was the very incarnation of Lord Ganesha himself, the elephant-headed god of beginnings. I have had many devotees tell me that when herds of wild elephants came upon the pilgrims on the way to the Ayyappan temple in the mountains, they would kneel the moment they saw Iyer's face, raise their trunks in reverence, and head back into the woods. Now he stood in front of the tree, with his eyes closed, overcome with devotion.

The crowd overflowed onto the cement road from both sides. No vehicle could pass by. The traffic from Vadaseri had to turn left at the clock tower and take a detour through Meenakshipuram to get to Kottar. People were laughing about how the contractor hired to cut down the tree had headed back to his town after writing to the municipality that there was no way he could complete his task now.

Later that evening, a meeting was held under the tamarind tree on the theme of "Protection of the Hindu dharma." Several scholars spoke, as did a few swamis. In that meeting—headed by Kambaramayanam Ananthan Pillai—Dhamu proclaimed that he was going to build an army of brave young men who would protect Hindu religion and Hindu gods from Muslims and Christians. He told the crowd that it was in the best interests of Muslims and Christians to refrain from hurting the religious sentiments of Hindus. But if they didn't, he said, all Hindus knew where the churches and mosques in town were, so they shouldn't force peace-loving Hindus to resort to violence.

People started saying that Dhamu had emerged victorious once again. Khader couldn't bear to hear everyone praising Dhamu's cunning and brilliance. He was distressed less by his defeat than by Dhamu's victory.

Once the tamarind tree became a deity, Chairman M. C. Joseph did not want to have anything to do with the issue. It was believed that the bishop sent for him and warned him against any further involvement. Copies of the *Travancore Nesan* were burned at every public rally. The government granted Isakki police protection at his request, and the offices of the *Travancore Nesan* were guarded by a twenty-four-hour police detail. Isakki's pen came to a screeching halt on the subject of the tamarind tree. However, just to show that he had not capitulated, Isakki still occasionally published letters that came in support of both sides of the issue. His friends said that the *Nesan*, which had previously sold three thousand copies, was now hitting the nine-thousand mark in the wake of the tamarind-tree crisis.

Khader alone was seething and fuming.

It was only a few days before the election. I still remember it very clearly. It was a Sunday. Market day. I had set out at the crack of dawn to buy a few things at the market. It was just starting to get hot when

I was on my way back home. I stopped for coffee at Ananda Bhavan Restaurant and was just stepping back out when I saw a few people running south from near the clock tower.

My first impression was that the whole street seemed to be strangely excited. I walked closer and asked somebody what was going on. Coolie Ayyappan lay stabbed under the tamarind tree, they said! I rushed back to the restaurant, left my bag of vegetables there for safekeeping, and ran toward the tamarind-tree junction.

The tree was completely surrounded by crowds. People at the back were pushing and shoving, trying to get closer.

By the time I arrived, coolie Ayyappan had already been carried away. Some said that he died only after he got to the government hospital and that the police had been able to record his statement before his life slipped away. Some said he was still holding on to his life by a thread.

Blood lay in congealed splotches beneath the tamarind tree. I could not help but lift my head and look at the silver face of the goddess. It looked to me like her green eyes had lowered their eyelids and she was looking at all the blood on the ground.

Nobody could make an informed guess as to who might have stabbed Ayyappan. But that did not stop wild speculations. Some said that it was all to do with a woman. One fellow said that he happened to know that Ayyappan had been taking treatment for venereal diseases, and he went into excruciating detail about this. Then there were others who said that the man who'd stabbed Ayyappan had not tried to escape, that he'd gone straight to the police station and turned himself in, and that it was on the basis of his information that the police had rushed to the spot, found Ayyappan on the brink of death, and taken him to the hospital. A few people were now on their way to the government hospital, running as fast as they could.

I went to the restaurant, picked up my bag, and went home. I washed up, ate my breakfast, and then set out on my bicycle to the police station, then to the government hospital, from there to the offices of the *Nesan*, and then on to the Thirteenth Ward, where Dhamu and Khader were contesting the election. Only then could I begin to get a sense of what had happened.

Both Dhamu and Khader were arrested that night, and the *Travancore Nesan* confirmed the news the next morning. The paper also published a portion of Khader's statement to the police.

People were shocked to learn from Khader's sworn testimony in court, which was later printed in the newspaper, that Ayyappan had approached Khader several days before he was stabbed under the tamarind tree. Khader had been sheltering him in his house with the hope that he might be able to use Ayyappan, when the time was right, to avenge himself against Dhamu.

Coolie Ayyappan had been in hiding and constantly on the move ever since he'd run from the police. Whenever he ran out of money, he came back to town and knocked on Dhamu's door in the middle of the night. At first, Dhamu did not hesitate to give him what he asked for, a hundred or two hundred rupees each time. But after a while, Dhamu started feeling that Ayyappan was hitting him up for money way too frequently, and he came to resent the man. Ayyappan also asked for a higher amount each time. Moreover, his tone had changed—he was not requesting money anymore; he was demanding it. Dhamu began to loathe the very sight of him, but he did not express it. The case against him regarding the vandalism of Khader's store sign was still on in court at the time, so he did not want to jeopardize his defense by antagonizing Ayyappan. However, every time Ayyappan came to him for money, he gave a little less than the amount asked. Eventually, when the case was dismissed due to lack of evidence, Dhamu's first reaction was immense relief that he could now stop wasting his money on keeping Ayyappan quiet.

The next time Ayyappan came to see him, Dhamu said: "Ayyappan, don't you think it's time for you to get yourself a job?"

"Who's going give a job to someone who goes to jail twice a year?"

"Well, you just have to try . . ."

"There's no point, even if I try."

"Not with that attitude."

"Why don't you give me a job, then? You can, if you want to."

Dhamu was silent.

"You see? Why would anyone else feel differently?"

Dhamu said nothing.

"I've ruined my life, listening to the likes of you. Now that people don't need me anymore, they've cast me away. But . . ."

Catching the shift in Ayyappan's tone and expression, Dhamu turned around before he could finish the sentence and walked back into the house.

When he came back out, there was an envelope in his hand.

"Look here," he said. "This time, I am giving you a bit more than usual. Don't drink it all away. Try to find somewhere to settle down, start a little shop, make a living. You cannot live forever on someone else's kindness."

Coolie Ayyappan said nothing in response. He took the money and left.

Not even two full months passed. One day, Dhamu returned home exhausted from all the election work and lay down for a nap. He had just drifted off to sleep when he heard a knock on the door.

It was coolie Ayyappan.

"You ungrateful dog! Get out of here!" shouted Dhamu. Ayyappan just stood there for a moment, fixing his unblinking eyes on Dhamu. His eyes grew bloodshot and the veins on his forehead throbbed. Even though he stood like a stone, there was a hint of a smile on his lips. Then he suddenly whipped his head around and left.

He stayed in town for the next two days, just wandering around. He picked up news of the elections and the disputes about the tamarind tree. He also understood that Dhamu was relishing the victory he had gained by turning the tamarind tree into a deity.

Ayyappan's brain worked fast. He realized it was the perfect time for him to approach Khader. At midnight, he knocked on Khader's door.

Khader said in court that he had agreed to offer Ayyappan refuge in his house because he had claimed he could make the tree die right on the spot in exchange for Khader's support.

Coolie Ayyappan was very diligent with his planning and execution. He knew that as election day approached, Dhamu and his friends would be up all night keeping vigil against the opposition trying to split up Dhamu's voting blocs, so all their attention would be on the constituency. Coolie Ayyappan therefore deliberately picked a day close to the election to carry out his plan.

He climbed up the tree at one in the morning. In the folds of his veshti, he carried a little bottle of mercury mixed with poison, which he had procured from a local healer. He took out his knife and gouged a hole in the tree where the trunk split into branches. He poured the potion into the hole, then plugged it with some cow dung he had brought in a banana-leaf packet. If he had heard so much as a whisper then, he wouldn't have tried to climb down the tree. But he was already halfway down the trunk when tragedy struck. He was suddenly blinded by a light in his eyes. He jumped to the ground and tried to run away, but three men pounced on him and pinned him to the earth. Coolie Ayyappan took out his penknife and held it up, over their heads. But one of the men grabbed his hand, wrested the knife away, and stabbed him in the chest with it. It was only a small wound, but the doctors at the government hospital said that the knife had punctured an artery—the injury was fatal.

Dhamu had sent three campaign workers on their bicycles to buy tea and snacks for everyone working through the night at the campaign office. They had been on their way back from the clock tower when they'd seen Ayyappan climbing down the tree.

After it was published in the newspapers that coolie Ayyappan had been stabbed to death and that he had poisoned the tree, hundreds of people

185

gathered at the tamarind tree. The devotees called in healers, who tried their best to administer urgent medicinal remedies to break the effects of the poison coursing through the tree. Many of these devotees did not leave the spot for hours.

There was no visible change in the tree on the first day. But by the next morning, it was clear to everyone that a dire transformation had occurred during the night. Lots of leaves had fallen. The lower branches were almost bare. In just a few days, even the smallest twigs had shed their leaves, and the tree stood completely naked. On the fourth day, a healer came and examined the tree by stripping a piece of bark from the trunk. No sap oozed out. "The tree is dead," he declared.

There were nearly five hundred people standing around the tree at the time. As soon as the healer pronounced the tree dead, an elderly devotee jumped up as if he had entered a trance; he ran toward Khader's store in a frenzy, where he picked up a fistful of earth and threw it against the store's locked doors, screaming curses all the while. A mob followed him and threw stones at the doors. They then broke the shutters, rushed into the store, and tore the place apart. The store was set on fire. But the damage was minimal, because the police and the fire service arrived at the scene almost immediately. Since the rioters did not disperse despite repeated warnings, the police had to resort to the use of batons.

After this, fights broke out in different parts of town. We heard that some Muslims had been attacked in Kottar. From the news we kept receiving, it looked as if terrible communal violence was about to break out. The state imposed a curfew. But the very night the curfew came into effect, a gang of students attacked the office of the *Travancore Nesan*. Isakki was away at the hairstyling salon at the time, so thankfully he didn't get hurt.

In those weeks, police vans rushed through the streets every few minutes, their sirens blaring. Sepoys armed with batons stood guard at the junctions. It was nearly two weeks before the town returned to normal.

The tamarind tree at the junction stood wilted and desiccated. It was dead. Only its carcass remained, waiting to be hauled out. Any minute, a woodcutter might show up and start chopping the tree without drawing much attention from anyone.

It was no longer a tree, no longer a deity. Just a corpse.

Summer winds had started to blow. The tamarind tree still danced absurdly in the breeze despite having given up its life. It was a pitiful sight. Revolting even. The spot where the tree stood would soon become a void. It had been so many years since the sun's rays touched and danced on the ground at that spot! For nearly a hundred years, if not longer, the tree had turned light into shade, heat into coolness. But now it was done with its work.

The tree had made it through so many summers. Who could tell how much blazing heat and pouring rain the tree must have endured, how many hot summer gusts and chill north winds the tree must have withstood? Never once did it ever complain that it was too hot or too rainy.

The flood of 1890 was the stuff of legend. People still talked about how buffaloes the size of little elephants were swept away by the Pazhayar River. The pariah settlement in Therekalputhoor drifted in the waters like a temple float. The tamarind tree was very young then. And very small. For three days, it stood in water that came up to its neck—no murmurs, no complaints.

It had even survived the droughts of the last few years. Its body had shrunk, sheltering just a little life in its roots; it stood with its skinny limbs and branches stretched out, staring unblinkingly at the sky. Even then it betrayed no emotions.

The tree had witnessed so much, endured so much.

Surrounded by water, that spot had been an island when the tree was born. And all around it were fields that stretched to the horizon, holding up the curving arch of the sky. In those days, there weren't many people around the tree. Only occasional passersby. The tree had no inkling of the extent of the human sprawl in this world. It had no idea that all those people possessed their own unique minds. The cow-herd boys were its only friends. Their arrival always brought the tree some excitement. How animated they were, when they raced each other as they swam toward the tree! Didn't some of those boys carve their symbols on the tree to mark their names? But those symbols had vanished without a trace over the years—and how cruelly time had marked those boys . . . Today, some of them could not walk without the aid of a stick; others saw their vision cloud over. Many even needed to mash the betel leaves before putting them in their mouths! And so many of them had already bade farewell to this world . . .

Indeed, so much time had passed.

"If you really wish to wipe off the mark of auspiciousness from a married woman's forehead, then go ahead and kill that tree." That was what Kambaramayanam Ananthan Pillai had dramatically told the town council. And he was right. For anyone who had seen the tamarind tree in its days of glory even once, the junction now wore a vacant and desolate look that indeed brought to their minds the image of a lonely widow. They were gripped with a longing for a wealth they had lost but had no hope of regaining ever again.

After the tamarind tree had been cut down, for as long as I stayed in town, I could not pass by the spot without being assailed by a terrible sense of emptiness. I believe many others in town were subjected to the same feelings. Even today, long after the tamarind tree is dead and gone, the place is still called the tamarind-tree junction. Our tongues had gotten used to that name. People could not forget it. That lingering habit is the only memorial to the life of the tamarind tree. The tree might have lost its very form, but its name was indestructible.

Whether people visit the junction or pass by the spot on their way to somewhere else, as long as they are people from our town, they find themselves wondering at some point, "Why was the tamarind tree destroyed?" Their minds will have to work hard to get to the truth, rejecting every easy answer that is sure to come up in their hearts. Will their minds ever find an answer that their souls can embrace whole-heartedly? God alone knows. But then, so what if they never arrive at such an answer? It would not be the end of the world. All we need is an honest question. One honest question would be worth a thousand answers. Besides, there is no harm in having to think these things through from time to time.

Khader's store closed down. The court handed him a prison sentence and he spent it at the Thiruvananthapuram Central Jail. His wife and children moved to Kalakkad.

Dhamu was released, but he came out dispirited. Perhaps it was the series of unfortunate incidents that had occurred, or his defeat in the election, or some other reason that lay buried deep within him, but he decided to leave town. He and his brother Chellappan sold the store and moved back home to Kuzhithurai with their wife and kids. Years later, when I happened to be in town, I heard that he had scraped some money together and started a dairy farm.

The winds changed direction in the Thirteenth Ward when both Khader and Dhamu were arrested before the election. Grandpa Peanut made the most of that opportunity. He went up to every voter and asked them not to vote for criminals. The voters were already disenchanted with Dhamu and Khader—and the two men's endless disputes over the tamarind tree certainly did not help matters.

Grandpa Peanut won a sweeping victory.

Women stood on the front steps to relish the sight of him setting out to his first meeting at the municipal council. The children came all the way up to the cement road to wave him goodbye.

The new shirt and dhoti that the old man wore on that day got dirty within a week. He washed and dried them every night and wore the same clothes to the council meeting the next morning.

All the money left over from the election campaign was gone in just a few months. But it has to be said that, in those few months, he and his family really did enjoy their lives. His grandchildren wore nice clothes for a while. His son shopped every day at the fish market. The family bought two goats so they'd have a supply of milk for the infants. Also, new pots and pans for the house. The old man gave up beedis and started smoking cigarettes.

Days of contentment are so few and far between in life. They slip away from us so fast!

Perhaps because the daily wash took its toll, his new clothes frayed quite fast. Holes appeared even in his double-fold veshti. Some of the pots and pans had to be pawned to make ends meet. When he returned home from council meetings, the hungry bawling of the children tormented his ears.

One morning, the old man dug out and dusted off his old candy box.

When he arrived at the madrassa entrance the next morning, bare-chested, a bell in his left hand and the candy box perched on his turban, children came running to him and surrounded him, delirious with joy, yelling, "Grandpa Peanut's back! He's back!"

Grandpa Peanut stared blankly at the faces of the children. Then his face broke into a smile. His eyes welled up with tears.

AFTERWORD

By S. R. Sundaram and
Thaila Ramanujam

On the novel

When our father Sundara Ramaswamy (SuRaa) wrote *Oru Puliyamarathin Kathai* (*The Tamarind Tree*), our country's reins were in the firm hands of Jawaharlal Nehru, India's first prime minister. By the time the novel was published in 1966, two years after Nehru's death, secularism was the uncontested ideal of the Indian state. However, while the novel deals with larger themes of modernity and secularism, it is deeply informed by a regional peculiarity: the story plays out in a region of India where Christians and Muslims outnumber Hindus. This is uncommon in a nation in which Hindus constitute over eighty percent of the population. In the 1960s, political Hinduism did not have a strong electoral foothold at the center or in the states. Hindutva, the ideology of Hindu nationalism, was not a major player in public life, except in the states bordering Pakistan, an Islamic nation-state carved out of British India.

Yet, the novel is prescient about the realities of India today—an India that bears little resemblance to the India of Nehru. The novel anticipates the popular appeal of Hindu narratives and aesthetics in politics. It indicates that the majority can develop a minority complex of being oppressed and victimized in their own country. It narrates the triumph of popular beliefs over the laws of the land and exposes the cynical politics espoused by religious, rightwing fanatics to gain power. It is also a story of how the media shapes narratives, promotes alternative truths, and exploits social fault lines for its own benefit—in the novel, when a municipal chairman and a local tabloid conspire to cut down a majestic tree at the center of the town, in a cynical ploy to win elections, they pave the way for the "arrival" of Hindutva forces. These are issues that are at the center of public life in India today. But not just in India. These concerns have a global appeal today; they speak to the central concerns of many liberal democracies, including the US and UK.

In the novel, faith-based manipulation reigns supreme over even the ill-conceived decisions of democratically elected bodies, as represented in this instance by the local municipal council, just like in contemporary India, where the Supreme Court is widely perceived to have placed the faith of the Hindus over the facts of the case and the laws of the land in the controversial 2019 judgment on the Ayodhya dispute. Hindu nationalists have long claimed that the Babri Masjid, a mosque built in Ayodhya during the reign of the first Mughal emperor, Babur, in the sixteenth century, was previously the site of a temple to the Hindu god Ram. This gave rise to a massive Hindu populist movement in the 1980s and led to a rogue demolition of the mosque in 1992. The resulting riots, which spread across north India, deeply divided Indian society along communal lines and eventually catapulted a Hindu nationalist party, the BJP, to power in India. The Supreme Court's judgment on Ayodhya, foregrounding faith over facts, has now led to several other such disputes claiming the rights of Hindus over mosques and Islamic monuments.

When Ananthan Pillai, a character in the novel, powerfully speaks for the public at the municipal council meeting where the cutting of the tamarind tree is up for debate, his voice could well be the voice of any "sober" Hindutva politician today:

"This town is a holy place, and the tamarind tree is sacred to it," he said. "The tree might be mute, it might also be maimed, but it is still a living thing."

When Dhamu proclaims in a meeting "that he was going to build an army of brave young men who would protect Hindu religion and Hindu gods from Muslims and Christians. He told the crowd that it was in the best interests of Muslims and Christians to refrain from hurting the religious sentiments of Hindus. But if they didn't, he said, all Hindus knew where the churches and mosques in town were, so they shouldn't force peace-loving Hindus to resort to violence," he could very well be echoing the views of any number of the Hindutva demagogues who are now powerful ministers in the central and state governments.

This continued relevance to changing political and social situations is perhaps why *Oru Puliyamarathin Kathai* continues to top the Tamil literature sales charts every year, over five decades after its publication.

On the translation

As overseers of the translation process, our only qualification being we are the children of the late author Sundara Ramaswamy, we ran into some thorny considerations.

We had no difficulty agreeing that any piece of creative work is an implicit contract between a reader and an author. If all goes well, within the first few pages of the book, an equilibrium of understanding is achieved between the two parties about the journey they are both about to embark on. A dynamic of mutual expectation emerges: about the author's commitment to forging an intimate communication through his written words and the reader's willingness to travel along to meet the author on his or her terms.

In a translated work, however, this sort of an implied understanding between the reader and the writer takes on another layer of complexity as both parties are primed by their own cultural milieus, their moral norms, and their varying styles of communication, not to mention the myriad assumptions they hold about the zeitgeist of the times they are embedded in.

The Tamarind Tree posed some specific concerns in addition. In our shared task of shaping the text, we found a translator in Aniruddhan, whose commitment and spirit and dedication was to preserve the original text as much as possible but worked tirelessly with us to make some adjustments when absolutely called for.

The first four chapters revolve around the tales told by a local maverick Asan. In these chapters, we see the birth of a town and get to know the tamarind tree as an intimate character in the book. However, starting with the fifth chapter, a whole new cast of characters emerge, taking the reader through labyrinthine political power plays and the overarching theme of this book: a town's growth and untimely decay caused by human avarice as witnessed in silence by a sprawling tamarind tree.

Other moments in the text called for clarifications in the form of adjudication with a foreign reader. For instance, a simple shaking of the head or a body gesture might mean one thing in the everyday semiotics of Tamil culture, but the same gesture might come to imply something entirely opposite in other cultures or have no significance at all. Based on the dialect or an idiomatic phraseology, a character who is not formally introduced in the beginning of a chapter might be instantly recognizable to a Tamil reader. But a foreign reader might miss this and would need to wait until the end of the chapter to be formally introduced to the same character. All of this character's nuanced communication skills and delightful interactions would be missed along the way.

In short, it fell on our shoulders to renegotiate a contract with the new reader on the author's behalf. How do we stay true to the original text, yet add guideposts to clarify intents and purposes in the author's absence? We found ourselves in the unenviable situation of trying to imagine what the author might have done had he been presented with such a dilemma.

In making decisions to add editorial changes without losing the nuanced work our father so magnificently achieves in his native language, and without losing fidelity to the original text, we were informed by and drew comfort from our shared knowledge of our father's approach to being accessible to the reader. We knew that our father, SuRaa, was so committed to establishing a strong link with his readers that he was amenable to editorial changes pointed out by his editors. One of us (Thaila) also vividly remembers conversations with our father during his visits to her home in Santa Cruz where they discussed and systematically studied the craft of writing—there were lengthy conversations and exercises and annotations on how to rope a reader in, where to favor nuanced subtlety, and where to compromise toward better transparency and easy accessibility.

We also remember that SuRaa's views of the editorial process changed dramatically over the years. He first submitted *Oru Puliyamarathin Kathai* to an iconic Tamil publishing house by the name of Vasagar Vattam. But he withdrew the work when they wanted to edit it. However, his attitude toward editing changed by the time he wrote his second novel. He worked with a team of editors assigned by the publisher (Cre-A), combing through the text line by line and carrying out the revisions he approved. He later described the process as shattering but enriching nevertheless. He revised his first novel again in the mid-1990s when someone pointed out an error in its timeline.

This intimate knowledge of our father's approach to writing and editing allows us to believe that our father would have been willing to make some adjustments to his text to reach any reader who was willing to take this journey with him. He would have wanted to convene with new readers from the world over. In making our father's dream and our dream of making this book available to a wider readership come true, we are grateful for the unwavering support we received from Gabi, Aniruddhan, and Tashan and Jayapriya.

Thaila Ramanujam
May 20, 2022
Santa Cruz

S. R. Sundaram (Kannan)
Nagercoil

ABOUT THE AUTHOR

Photo © 2002 Puduvai Ilavenil

Sundara Ramaswamy was one of the most versatile and innovative of Tamil writers. A modernist and dazzling stylist, he wrote in many genres, including poetry, fiction, theater, essays, and literary criticism. In addition to his path-breaking novels, Sundara also edited and published the magazine *Kalachuvadu*, which was a notable forum for new writing and literary debate.

ABOUT THE TRANSLATOR

Aniruddhan Vasudevan is an award-winning translator, performer, writer, and anthropologist. He is currently a Cotsen Postdoctoral Fellow at the Princeton Society of Fellows, Princeton University. Among his translations are works of fiction by such celebrated Tamil authors as Ambai and Perumal Murugan.